DETECTIVE GIRL AND THE MISSING CHILD

By
Humayun

Introducing Detective Girl
Meeting the Family
Investigating the Scene
Chasing Down Leads
A New Clue Emerges
A Break in the Case
A Rescue Mission
Reuniting the Family
Celebrating the Victory
Back to Reality
New Challenges
Discovering New Clues
Building a Case
Closing In
Solving the Case
Moving Forward
Conclusion

INTRODUCING DETECTIVE GIRL

The sun was just starting to set over the city as Detective Girl made her way through the bustling streets. She was on her way to the precinct to start her new case, and she was feeling excited and a little nervous.

As she walked into the building, she was greeted by the familiar sights and sounds of the station. Officers rushed back and forth, phones rang off the hook, and the occasional shout echoed through the halls.

Detective Girl made her way to her new office, a small but cozy space with a desk, a few chairs, and a bookshelf filled with crime novels. She took a deep breath and sat down, ready to begin her work.

But before she got started on the case at hand, Detective Girl took a moment to reflect on how she got here. She had always been drawn to the world of crime and mystery, ever since she was a little girl. She would spend hours poring over detective novels and watching crime shows on TV, fascinated by the complex web of clues and suspects that made up each case.

As she grew older, Detective Girl knew that she wanted to make a difference in the world by helping to solve real-life crimes. She went to school to study criminology and criminal justice, and eventually landed a job at the police department.

Over the years, Detective Girl had made a name for herself as a talented and tenacious investigator. She was known for her sharp mind, her attention to detail, and her ability to get to the heart of even the most challenging cases.

And now, here she was, starting a new case that would put all her skills to the test. A child had gone missing, and it was up to Detective Girl to find out what happened and bring them home safely.

With a sense of purpose and determination, Detective Girl got to work. She knew that this case would be a tough one, but she was ready for the challenge. She would do whatever it took to find the missing child and bring them back to their family.

Detective Girl glanced around her office, taking in the familiar sights and sounds of her workspace. The room was dimly lit, with only a small lamp casting a soft glow across her desk. The walls were adorned with pictures of her family, colleagues, and friends, reminding her of the people who had supported her on her journey.

As she sat there, lost in thought, Detective Girl couldn't help but feel a sense of pride in all she had accomplished. She had solved some of the most challenging cases in the city, bringing justice to victims and their families. But she knew that with every new case came new challenges and obstacles to overcome.

The case of the missing child would be no exception. Detective Girl knew that time was of the essence when it came to missing children, and that every second counted. She had to act fast to gather clues, follow leads, and find the missing child before it was too late.

With a deep breath, Detective Girl stood up from her desk and made her way to the squad room. She knew that her colleagues would be eager to hear about her new case, and she was ready to collaborate with them to bring the missing child home.

As she walked through the halls of the precinct, Detective Girl couldn't help but feel a sense of camaraderie with her fellow officers. They were all working towards the same goal: to protect and serve their community. And she knew that together, they could accomplish great things.

As she entered the squad room, Detective Girl was greeted by a chorus of greetings and well-wishes from her colleagues. They all knew that she was one of the best investigators on the force, and they were eager to work with her on the new case.

Over the next few hours, Detective Girl worked with her team to gather information, interview witnesses, and follow leads. It was slow going at first, but with each new piece of evidence they uncovered, the case began to take shape.

As she worked, Detective Girl couldn't help but feel a sense of purpose and determination. She knew that this case was important, not just for the missing child and their family, but for the community as a whole. And she was determined to do whatever it took to bring the missing child home safe and sound.

With her colleagues by her side, Detective Girl felt confident that they would be able to crack the case. She knew that it wouldn't be easy, but she was ready for the challenge. And she knew that, no matter what, she would always put the safety and well-being of the people she served above all else.

As Detective Girl delved deeper into the missing child case, she couldn't help but take note of the setting and time period. The case was set in a bustling city in the present day, but it was clear that there were certain aspects of the city that were unique to this time period.

The city was a sprawling metropolis, with towering skyscrapers, bustling streets, and a diverse mix of people from all walks of life. Detective Girl had lived in the city her whole life, and she knew it like the back of her hand. But as she walked the streets now, she couldn't help but feel a sense of unease. Something was different, something had changed.

As she pondered this, Detective Girl couldn't help but think back to the history of the city. It had been founded over two hundred years ago, and had grown and evolved over the centuries. Each decade had brought new changes, new challenges, and new opportunities. But there had always been a sense of continuity, of connection to the past.

But now, as Detective Girl walked the streets of the city, she felt a sense of disconnect. The modern world was moving at a breakneck pace, and it seemed as though the city was struggling to keep up. Buildings were being torn down and replaced with new ones at an alarming rate, and the cultural and historical landmarks that had once defined the city were disappearing.

Despite this, Detective Girl remained determined to solve the case at hand. She knew that the city, for all its flaws and imperfections, was still a place where people could come together, help one another, and work towards a better future.

And so, with a sense of purpose and determination, Detective Girl continued her investigation. She combed through the city's streets, alleys, and neighborhoods, following leads and gathering evidence. And as she worked, she couldn't help but feel a sense of connection to the city and its people.

In the end, Detective Girl's hard work paid off. She was able to track down the missing child and bring them home safely to their family. And as she stood on the steps of the police station, surrounded by her colleagues and members of the community, Detective Girl couldn't help but feel a sense of pride and hope. She knew that, no matter what challenges lay ahead, she and the people of the city would always come together to protect and serve one another.

As Detective Girl continued to investigate, she began to notice more details about the city and its time period. She saw how technology had advanced and changed the way people lived and interacted with one another. Smartphones and social media were ubiquitous, and people communicated in ways that would have been unimaginable just a few decades earlier.

But with these advancements came new challenges. Detective Girl found that people were often more disconnected from one another, even as they were more connected than ever before. And she saw how social media and technology could be used to deceive, manipulate, and harm others.

As she delved deeper into the case, Detective Girl also became aware of the city's social and economic disparities. She saw how wealth and privilege were concentrated in certain neighborhoods, while others were plagued by poverty, crime, and neglect. She saw how these disparities affected the lives of the people who lived in the city, and how they could contribute to the challenges of finding a missing child.

Despite these challenges, Detective Girl remained determined to solve the case and bring the missing child home. She knew that the city had its problems, but she also saw the resilience and strength of its people. She saw how members of the community came together to support one another in times of crisis, and how they worked to make the city a better place for all.

In the end, Detective Girl's investigation led her to a suspect who had abducted the missing child. With the help of her colleagues, she was able to apprehend the suspect and bring them to justice. The missing child was reunited with their family, and the city breathed a collective sigh of relief.

As Detective Girl reflected on the case, she realized that it had taught her a lot about the city and its time period. She saw both the good and the bad, the challenges and the opportunities. And she knew that, no matter what the future held, she would always be committed to serving the people of the city, and doing her best to make it a safer, more just, and more connected place for all.

It was a warm summer day when Detective Girl received the call. A child had gone missing, and she was the lead detective on the case. As she listened to the details, her heart sank. She knew that finding a missing child was one of the most challenging and emotional cases she could face.

As she arrived at the scene, Detective Girl saw the distraught parents and the growing crowd of concerned neighbors. She knew that time was of the essence, and that every minute that passed could make the difference between finding the child alive and well, or not at all.

The central conflict of the story was set. Detective Girl was on the case, determined to use all of her skills and resources to bring the missing child home safely. She knew that the clock was ticking, and that she had to act quickly and decisively to find any leads or clues that could help in the search.

But the case was not going to be easy. The city was vast, and there were countless places where the missing child could be. Detective Girl had to work with her team of detectives and police officers to cover as much ground as possible, interviewing witnesses, reviewing surveillance footage, and searching for any evidence that could help in the investigation.

As Detective Girl continued to work on the case, she found herself struggling with the weight of the responsibility. She knew that the missing child's life was in her hands, and that the outcome of the case could have a lasting impact on the child and their family.

But she was determined to succeed. She was driven by her compassion for the missing child and their family, as well as her commitment to upholding justice and protecting the most vulnerable members of society.

And so, with a sense of urgency and purpose, Detective Girl continued to work tirelessly on the case. She knew that the challenges would be great, but she also knew that she had the skills, the determination, and the support of her colleagues to see the case through to its conclusion.

As Detective Girl delved deeper into the case, she began to uncover more information that complicated the investigation.

She learned that the missing child had been involved in a custody battle between their parents, and that there were several people who had a motive to take the child.

Detective Girl had to navigate the complexities of the custody battle, working with lawyers and court officials to gather more information about the case. She also had to interview family members and friends, trying to piece together a picture of the missing child's life and relationships.

As the investigation continued, Detective Girl found herself working long hours, sacrificing her own personal life to focus on the case. But she was driven by her determination to find the missing child and bring them home.

The central conflict of the story continued to build, as Detective Girl faced setbacks and challenges along the way. There were dead ends and false leads, moments of frustration and despair. But through it all, she remained focused on the task at hand, using her skills and experience to stay one step ahead of the perpetrator.

Finally, after weeks of intense investigation, Detective Girl and her team uncovered a crucial clue that led them to the missing child. The child had been taken to a remote location outside the city, hidden away by someone who had wanted to keep them out of sight.

With the help of her colleagues, Detective Girl was able to locate the child and bring them back to their family. There were tears of joy and relief as the child was reunited with their loved ones, and the community breathed a collective sigh of relief.

In the end, Detective Girl's determination and skill had won out, and the central conflict of the story had been resolved. But she knew that the impact of the case would stay with her for a long time to come, reminding her of the importance of her work, and the value of every life she had the chance to save.

MEETING THE FAMILY

As Detective Girl worked tirelessly on the case, she knew that one of the most important steps was to establish a connection with the family of the missing child. She understood that the family would be going through an unimaginable amount of pain and fear, and that her role was not just to solve the case, but also to offer support and comfort to those affected.

One afternoon, Detective Girl arranged to meet with the family of the missing child. As she walked up to their front door, she felt a mix of nervousness and compassion. She knew that her words and actions would have a significant impact on the family's well-being, and that every gesture of support could make a difference.

As she entered the family's home, she was met with a mixture of emotions. The parents were visibly distraught, struggling to hold back tears as they told Detective Girl about their missing child. Detective Girl listened carefully, taking notes and asking questions, trying to get a clear picture of what had happened and how she could help.

She knew that the family needed answers, but she also knew that they needed reassurance that everything possible was being done to find their child. She made a promise to the family that she would do everything in her power to bring the child back home safely, and that she would keep them updated on every step of the investigation.

Over the next few days, Detective Girl visited the family regularly, offering updates on the case and answering any questions they had. She also spent time talking with the family, getting to know them as people and offering her support in any way she could.

As she spent time with the family, Detective Girl began to feel a personal connection with them. She saw their pain and fear firsthand, and it strengthened her resolve to solve the case and bring their child home.

In the end, the connection that Detective Girl established with the family would play a critical role in the investigation. It allowed her to understand the family's needs and concerns, and to work more effectively with them to solve the case. It also reminded her of the human impact of her work, and the importance of approaching every case with empathy and compassion.

As Detective Girl spent more time with the family, she learned more about the missing child's personality and interests. She saw pictures of the child's artwork and toys, and listened to stories about their favorite activities and hobbies.

These details helped Detective Girl form a more complete picture of the child's life, which would later prove valuable in her investigation. She was able to identify potential leads and suspects based on the child's relationships and interests, and she could better understand the emotional impact of the situation on the family.

At the same time, Detective Girl's interactions with the family also had an emotional impact on her. She felt a deep sense of empathy and concern for the family, and she was determined to do everything in her power to bring their child home.

As the investigation progressed, Detective Girl continued to work closely with the family, providing updates and answering questions. She also took extra steps to ensure that the family felt supported and cared for, arranging counseling services and other resources to help them cope with their trauma.

In the end, Detective Girl's connection with the family proved to be a critical factor in the investigation's success. It allowed her to gain insights and information that would not have been possible otherwise, and it gave the family the comfort and reassurance they needed during a difficult time. It also reminded Detective Girl of the human impact of her work, and reinforced her commitment to serving her community with compassion and dedication.

As Detective Girl continued to investigate the case, she knew that one of the most important steps was to learn more about the missing child's background and personality. She understood that every detail about the child could be valuable in solving the case and bringing the child back home.

She began by interviewing the child's teachers, classmates, and friends. She asked questions about the child's behavior, interests, and relationships, trying to get a complete picture of who the child was and what their life was like.

Through these interviews, Detective Girl learned that the child was a bright and creative student, who loved to draw and paint. They were also a passionate soccer player, and often played with their friends after school.

However, Detective Girl also uncovered some disturbing information. She learned that the child had been the victim of bullying at school, and had been experiencing anxiety and depression as a result. She also discovered that the child's parents had been going through a difficult divorce, which had caused significant stress and tension at home.

As Detective Girl dug deeper into the child's background and personality, she began to see how these factors could be connected to the child's disappearance. She hypothesized that the stress and anxiety the child was experiencing, along with the bullying at school, could have led them to run away or seek refuge somewhere else.

With this new understanding, Detective Girl and her team began to explore new leads and search areas. They checked local parks, abandoned buildings, and other places that the child may have been drawn to.

Through tireless work and determination, Detective Girl and her team were finally able to locate the missing child, who had been hiding in an abandoned building near the school. The child was reunited with their family, and Detective Girl was able to use her understanding of the child's personality and background to help provide the support and resources the child needed to heal from their traumatic experience.

In the end, Detective Girl's commitment to learning about the child's background and personality proved to be a critical factor in solving the case. By taking the time to understand who the child was and what they were going through, she was able to connect the dots and find the missing piece of the puzzle. It was a reminder of the importance of empathy and compassion in detective work, and of the power of understanding people's stories to make a difference in their lives.

After the child was found and reunited with their family, Detective Girl continued to work closely with them to ensure that they received the support they needed. She arranged for the child to receive counseling and other resources to help them cope with the emotional trauma of the experience.

Through her interactions with the family, Detective Girl also learned more about the impact that the child's disappearance had on them. She saw firsthand the fear and anxiety that the family had experienced, and the relief and joy that came with the child's safe return.

As Detective Girl reflected on the case, she realized that her understanding of the child's background and personality had been crucial in solving the case. It allowed her to see beyond the surface-level details of the case and to understand the complex emotional factors that had led to the child's disappearance.

It also reminded her of the importance of empathy and compassion in detective work. By taking the time to understand the child and their family, she was able to provide them with the support and resources they needed to heal from the experience.

In the end, Detective Girl's commitment to understanding the child's background and personality was a testament to her dedication to serving her community. It was a reminder that every case is more than just a set of facts and evidence; it is a story about people's lives and experiences, and the role that detectives can play in helping them find justice and healing.

With a deeper understanding of the missing child's background and personality, Detective Girl began to develop leads on where the child might have gone. She knew that every minute was critical in a missing child case, and that she needed to act quickly to find the child and bring them home safely.

She started by analyzing all of the evidence and information she had gathered so far. She looked for patterns, connections, and potential leads, trying to piece together a picture of where the child might be.

One of the first places Detective Girl looked was the child's school. She interviewed the child's teachers, classmates, and friends, asking if they had seen or heard anything unusual on the day the child went missing. She also looked for signs of disturbance or forced entry, trying to determine if the child had been taken against their will.

Another lead Detective Girl pursued was the child's online activity. She knew that children today spend a lot of time on social media and other online platforms, and that this could be a valuable source of information. She checked the child's social media accounts and online activity, looking for any clues about where they might have gone or who they might have been with.

As she continued to follow these leads, Detective Girl also made sure to stay in close contact with the child's family. She knew that they could provide valuable insights and information, and that keeping them informed and involved in the investigation was critical to finding the child.

Through her tireless work and dedication, Detective Girl was finally able to develop a solid lead on where the child might be. She received a tip from a local resident who had seen a child matching the missing child's description in a nearby park.

Detective Girl and her team immediately sprang into action, rushing to the park to investigate. They combed the area, searching for any sign of the missing child. After a tense few hours, they finally found the child hiding in a nearby bush.

The child was cold, hungry, and scared, but otherwise unharmed. Detective Girl and her team quickly wrapped the child in a blanket and took them to the hospital for a check-up. The child was soon reunited with their family, who were overjoyed to have them back safe and sound.

As Detective Girl reflected on the case, she realized that her ability to develop and follow leads was critical in solving the case. It allowed her to make progress even in the face of overwhelming odds and to never give up hope in finding the missing child.

Detective Girl's success in developing leads was also a testament to her experience and expertise as a detective. She knew how to look for clues and evidence, how to analyze information, and how to connect the dots to create a clear picture of what had happened.

At the same time, Detective Girl never lost sight of the fact that every missing child case is unique. She understood that each case requires a different approach and that there is no one-size-fits-all solution.

This was especially true in the case of the missing child. Detective Girl had to use all of her skills and resources to follow every lead, analyze every piece of evidence, and leave no stone unturned in the search for the child.

Through her dedication and hard work, Detective Girl was able to bring the missing child home safely. Her success was not just a victory for her, but for the entire community. It showed that even in the most challenging of cases, justice and safety can be achieved with the right combination of skill, expertise, and compassion.

As Detective Girl continued to reflect on the case, she knew that she would always carry the lessons she learned with her. She knew that every case was an opportunity to learn and grow as a detective and as a human being, and that there was always more to discover about the world around her.

For Detective Girl, the missing child case was a reminder of the importance of never giving up hope, of always following leads, and of working tirelessly to bring justice and safety to those in need. It was a lesson that she knew would guide her through every case she worked on in the future.

INVESTIGATING THE SCENE

With a solid lead in hand, Detective Girl decided to visit the location where the missing child was last seen. She knew that this was a critical part of the investigation, as it would give her a chance to gather firsthand information about the child's disappearance and to assess the scene for any potential evidence.

As Detective Girl arrived at the location, she took in everything around her. She noted the time of day, the weather, the lighting, and the overall atmosphere of the area. She also spoke to witnesses who had seen the child last, asking them about what they had observed and whether they had noticed anything unusual.

As she examined the scene, Detective Girl began to piece together a timeline of events leading up to the child's disappearance. She checked for signs of struggle or disturbance, and looked for any potential clues that might have been left behind.

Detective Girl also worked with her team to gather surveillance footage from the area, hoping to catch a glimpse of the missing child or anyone who might have been involved in their disappearance. She checked local stores and other businesses for any footage that might be helpful, and interviewed anyone who might have seen something.

Through her careful examination of the scene, Detective Girl was able to gather valuable information that would help her move the case forward. She discovered a discarded piece of clothing that matched the missing child's description, and was able to use it as evidence to help identify potential suspects.

As she left the scene, Detective Girl felt a renewed sense of determination. She knew that every piece of information she had gathered would bring her closer to solving the case and finding the missing child.

Reflecting on the experience, Detective Girl realized the importance of visiting the last known location in any missing person case. It was a critical step in the investigation, allowing her to gather valuable information and assess the scene for any potential evidence.

At the same time, she understood that this was just one part of a much larger investigation. There were still many questions that needed to be answered and many leads that needed to be followed. But with each new piece of information, Detective Girl was one step closer to bringing the missing child home safely.

As Detective Girl continued to analyze the evidence and information she had gathered from the last known location, she began to notice certain patterns and inconsistencies. She realized that some witnesses had provided conflicting statements, and that there were some pieces of evidence that did not seem to fit together.

This led Detective Girl to dig deeper into the investigation, examining each piece of evidence and re-interviewing witnesses to get a better understanding of what had happened. She worked tirelessly, often spending long hours in the office and at the scene, and refused to give up until she had found the answers she was looking for.

Finally, after weeks of hard work and dedication, Detective Girl was able to piece together the puzzle and uncover the truth behind the missing child case. She discovered that the child had been abducted by someone close to the family, and that they had been holding the child against their will in a remote location.

With the help of her team, Detective Girl was able to rescue the missing child and apprehend the perpetrator. It was a moment of triumph and relief, not just for Detective Girl, but for the entire community.

As she reflected on the case, Detective Girl knew that it was her determination and perseverance that had ultimately led to its successful resolution. She understood that every missing person case was unique, and that it required a unique approach and a deep understanding of the circumstances involved.

For Detective Girl, the missing child case was a reminder of the importance of never giving up, even in the face of seemingly insurmountable obstacles. It was a testament to the power of dedication, hard work, and perseverance, and to the importance of finding justice for those who had been wronged.

And with each new case she worked on, Detective Girl would carry these lessons with her, using them to guide her as she continued to seek out the truth and protect the innocent.

With the location of the last sighting in hand, Detective Girl set out to search for any additional clues or evidence that might help her solve the case. She knew that even the smallest detail could make a big difference in piecing together what had happened to the missing child.

First, Detective Girl searched the immediate area surrounding the last known location. She combed through the nearby streets, alleys, and buildings, looking for any signs of the missing child or any potential evidence that might have been left behind. She used her keen observational skills to identify even the smallest detail, such as a discarded piece of paper or a footprint on the ground.

Next, she expanded her search to nearby neighborhoods, talking to local residents and business owners to see if anyone had seen or heard anything suspicious. She also looked for any security cameras or other surveillance devices that might have captured useful footage of the missing child or anyone involved in their disappearance.

As she searched, Detective Girl made sure to carefully document any potential evidence, taking photos, videos, and notes to ensure that nothing was missed. She also worked with her team to analyze any evidence that was found, such as fingerprints, DNA, or other forensic clues, in order to determine whether it could be linked to the missing child or any potential suspects.

Throughout her search, Detective Girl remained focused and determined, knowing that every piece of evidence could be critical to the case. She worked tirelessly, often putting in long hours and sacrificing her personal time in order to ensure that nothing was missed.

Finally, after days of searching, Detective Girl was able to uncover a key piece of evidence that would help break the case wide open. She discovered a discarded item of clothing that was linked to a potential suspect, leading her and her team to a location where the missing child was being held captive.

As Detective Girl reflected on her search for clues and evidence, she realized that it was her attention to detail and her persistence that had led to the successful resolution of the case. She understood that in any investigation, it was critical to leave no stone unturned, and to be willing to follow every lead, no matter how small.

And with the missing child safely reunited with their family, Detective Girl knew that her hard work and dedication had made a real difference in the lives of those she had sworn to protect.

As Detective Girl continued her search, she encountered a number of obstacles and challenges that tested her resolve and pushed her skills to the limit. For example, she had to navigate complex social dynamics within the community, some of which were suspicious of outsiders and reluctant to cooperate with law enforcement.

In addition, Detective Girl had to contend with misleading or false information from potential witnesses or suspects, forcing her to use her intuition and analytical skills to discern the truth from lies. She also had to manage the emotional toll of working on a case involving a missing child, which required her to remain focused and professional even in the face of heartbreaking circumstances.

Despite these challenges, Detective Girl remained committed to the task at hand, never losing sight of her goal to find the missing child and bring them home safely. She used her training and experience to adapt to each new situation, constantly refining her techniques and strategies to optimize her search efforts.

Through her tireless work, Detective Girl was able to generate a number of potential leads and suspects, which she and her team methodically pursued. She conducted interviews, followed up on tips, and used a variety of forensic techniques to piece together a picture of what had happened to the missing child.

Overall, Detective Girl's dedication to the case and her unwavering commitment to justice and protecting the innocent were the driving forces behind her successful search for clues and evidence. Her resourcefulness, tenacity, and compassion served as an inspiration to those around her, and helped her to emerge as one of the most skilled and respected detectives in her department.

After collecting evidence and following up on leads, Detective Girl began conducting interviews with witnesses and potential suspects. She spoke to anyone who had seen or interacted with the missing child in the days leading up to their disappearance, as well as anyone who might have knowledge of their whereabouts.

During these interviews, Detective Girl used her natural charisma and interpersonal skills to build rapport with her subjects. She listened carefully to their stories, asking probing questions and following up on any inconsistencies or discrepancies in their accounts.

Through this process, Detective Girl was able to identify a number of individuals who could have been involved in the disappearance of the child. She developed a list of potential suspects, and began to narrow down the list through further investigation and analysis of the evidence.

As she continued to work on the case, Detective Girl faced a number of challenges in conducting these interviews. Some witnesses were hesitant to come forward, either because they were afraid of retribution or because they did not want to get involved in the investigation. Others provided misleading or incomplete information, forcing Detective Girl to use her intuition and analytical skills to determine the truth.

Despite these challenges, Detective Girl persisted in her efforts to gather information and uncover the truth. Through her dedication and hard work, she was able to identify the person responsible for the child's disappearance and bring them to justice.

Throughout the interview process, Detective Girl relied on her training, experience, and intuition to make important decisions and solve complex problems. Her ability to connect with people and gain their trust was a key factor in her success, as was her relentless pursuit of the truth and unwavering commitment to protecting the innocent.

As Detective Girl delved deeper into her interviews, she also began to uncover some unexpected information about the missing child and their family. She learned about their relationships, habits, and routines, and discovered some potential motives for why the child might have gone missing.

Through her interviews with witnesses and suspects, Detective Girl was also able to gain a deeper understanding of the local community, including its social dynamics and power structures. She learned about the various tensions and conflicts that existed within the community, and how these might have played a role in the child's disappearance.

In addition to conducting interviews, Detective Girl also worked closely with her team to analyze and interpret the evidence they had collected. They used a variety of techniques, such as forensic analysis and computer modeling, to reconstruct the events leading up to the child's disappearance and identify potential suspects.

As they worked on the case, Detective Girl and her team faced a number of challenges, including resistance from certain members of the community, limited resources, and political pressure to close the case quickly. Despite these obstacles, Detective Girl remained focused and determined, using her skills and expertise to push through each new challenge and get one step closer to finding the missing child.

In the end, Detective Girl's interviews played a critical role in solving the case and bringing the perpetrator to justice. Her persistence, dedication, and compassion helped her to uncover the truth, and her unwavering commitment to justice and protecting the innocent made her a hero in the eyes of the community.

CHASING DOWN LEADS

With her interviews completed, Detective Girl now had a better understanding of the potential suspects and leads in the case. She carefully analyzed the information she had gathered and began to prioritize her follow-up efforts.

One lead that had caught her attention was a tip from a witness who had seen a suspicious vehicle near the location where the child had last been seen. Detective Girl and her team worked tirelessly to track down the owner of the vehicle and gather any relevant information. After several days of investigation, they were finally able to identify a suspect who had ties to the local community.

Another lead that Detective Girl was pursuing was related to the child's online activity. Through her interviews with the child's friends and family, Detective Girl had learned that the child was active on several social media platforms. She worked with her team to analyze the child's online activity, looking for any clues or patterns that might help them locate the missing child.

As she followed up on these and other leads, Detective Girl encountered several challenges. Some of the suspects and witnesses she was working with were uncooperative or evasive, and some of the information she received was contradictory or incomplete. However, Detective Girl remained persistent, using her analytical skills and intuition to make sense of the information she had and uncover the truth.

As Detective Girl continued to work on the case, she also became more emotionally invested in finding the missing child. She developed a deep sense of empathy and compassion for the child's family and friends, and was determined to do whatever it took to bring the child home safely.

Despite the challenges and setbacks, Detective Girl remained focused on her goal. She knew that every lead and piece of information could be the key to solving the case, and she was determined to leave no stone unturned.

As Detective Girl followed up on leads, she also encountered new evidence that added to the complexity of the case. She and her team carefully analyzed the evidence, searching for any clues that might help them piece together what had happened to the missing child.

One piece of evidence that stood out was a surveillance video that had been captured near the location where the child had last been seen. Detective Girl and her team studied the footage, looking for any potential suspects or vehicles that might have been involved in the child's disappearance.

Through her follow-up efforts, Detective Girl also uncovered new information about the missing child's background and personality. She learned about the child's hobbies, interests, and relationships, and used this information to build a more complete picture of the child's life and potential motivations for running away.

As the case progressed, Detective Girl began to feel the weight of the responsibility she had taken on. She knew that the missing child's family and the community were counting on her to find answers and bring the perpetrator to justice. Despite the pressure, she remained focused and committed, determined to see the case through to its resolution.

As she followed up on leads and analyzed evidence, Detective Girl also worked closely with her team to develop new strategies and approaches to the case. They brainstormed ideas, shared information, and collaborated on new leads and potential suspects.

Through her persistence and hard work, Detective Girl began to piece together the puzzle of the missing child case. She identified potential suspects, analyzed evidence, and followed up on leads until she finally uncovered the truth behind the child's disappearance. Her dedication and perseverance made her a hero in the eyes of the community and brought a sense of closure to the missing child's family.

Armed with the new evidence and leads, Detective Girl and her team began to pursue potential suspects in the missing child case. They carefully analyzed the evidence, looking for any connections or patterns that might lead them to the person responsible for the child's disappearance.

One of the first suspects they pursued was a neighbor who had been seen acting suspiciously near the location where the child had last been seen. Detective Girl and her team carefully interviewed the neighbor and searched his property for any evidence that might link him to the crime.

Although they didn't find any concrete evidence, Detective Girl and her team remained suspicious of the neighbor and continued to investigate him. They monitored his activities and movements, looking for any signs of guilt or wrongdoing.

As they pursued potential suspects, Detective Girl and her team also reached out to the community for help. They asked for tips and information from anyone who might have seen something or heard something related to the missing child case.

Through their outreach efforts, they received several tips that led them to other potential suspects. Detective Girl and her team carefully followed up on each lead, gathering more evidence and information as they went.

As they pursued potential suspects, Detective Girl also remained mindful of the missing child's family and their need for answers. She communicated with them regularly, providing updates on the progress of the investigation and offering support and encouragement.

Despite facing numerous challenges and setbacks along the way, Detective Girl remained focused on her goal of finding the missing child and bringing the perpetrator to justice. Her unwavering determination and commitment to the case ultimately paid off, leading her to the breakthrough she needed to solve the case and reunite the missing child with their family.

As Detective Girl and her team pursued potential suspects, they encountered many obstacles and dead ends. Some suspects had alibis that checked out, while others seemed to have no connection to the missing child at all.

Despite these setbacks, Detective Girl remained determined and persevered. She and her team continued to analyze the evidence and follow up on leads, never giving up hope that they would find the missing child.

At one point, they received a tip that led them to a small town several miles away from where the child had gone missing. They discovered that a man matching the description of a suspect they had been pursuing had been seen in the area.

Detective Girl and her team quickly made their way to the town and began searching for the man. After several hours of searching, they finally located him in a run-down motel on the outskirts of town.

They carefully approached the man, who appeared nervous and agitated. Through careful questioning and interrogation, they were able to gather enough evidence to link him to the missing child case.

With the evidence they had gathered, Detective Girl and her team were able to make an arrest and bring the perpetrator to justice. The missing child was located unharmed and reunited with their family, who were overjoyed to have their child back home safe and sound.

For Detective Girl, the case was both challenging and rewarding. She had faced numerous obstacles and setbacks, but her unwavering determination and commitment to justice had ultimately paid off. The missing child case had been solved, and justice had been served.

As Detective Girl continued her investigation into the missing child case, she faced a number of roadblocks and challenges that tested her skills as a detective and her resolve to bring the missing child home safely.

One of the biggest challenges was the lack of information about the child's whereabouts. Despite following up on numerous leads and tips, Detective Girl and her team were unable to find any concrete evidence that would lead them to the missing child.

In addition to the lack of evidence, Detective Girl also encountered resistance from some of the potential witnesses and suspects they interviewed. Some people were unwilling to cooperate with the investigation or provided false information, making it difficult for Detective Girl to determine the truth.

Furthermore, Detective Girl had to navigate the complex dynamics of the missing child's family, who were understandably distraught and emotional. This made it difficult for her to get a clear picture of the child's background and the events leading up to their disappearance.

Despite these challenges, Detective Girl remained focused and determined. She worked tirelessly to gather as much information as possible, even if it meant going back to square one and starting over.

She also utilized her creativity and resourcefulness to overcome the obstacles in her path. She enlisted the help of other experts, such as forensic analysts and behavioral specialists, to gain additional insights into the case.

Through it all, Detective Girl remained dedicated to her mission of finding the missing child and bringing them home safely. Her unwavering commitment and perseverance ultimately helped her overcome the challenges and roadblocks in her path and led to a successful resolution of the case.

As the investigation continued, Detective Girl faced additional challenges that tested her limits. She encountered resistance from some members of the community who were suspicious of the police and didn't trust their investigation.

Furthermore, Detective Girl had to navigate the media's coverage of the case. She had to be careful about what information was released to the public, as well as how it was presented. This required her to balance the need for transparency with the need to protect the integrity of the investigation.

As she pursued potential suspects, Detective Girl also had to be mindful of her own safety. She worked closely with her team and followed proper protocol to ensure that they were all protected throughout the investigation.

Despite the challenges she faced, Detective Girl remained committed to her duty and to the missing child's family. She spent countless hours poring over evidence, interviewing witnesses, and following leads. Her persistence paid off when she finally uncovered a crucial piece of information that led her to the missing child's whereabouts.

Through her resourcefulness and dedication, Detective Girl was able to bring the missing child home safely and reunite them with their family. Her success in solving the case earned her the respect and admiration of her colleagues and the community, and cemented her reputation as a skilled and determined detective.

A NEW CLUE EMERGES

As Detective Girl and her team continued their investigation into the missing child case, they had hit a dead end. Despite following up on numerous leads and tips, they were unable to find any concrete evidence that would lead them to the missing child.

However, one day, Detective Girl stumbled upon a new clue that could crack the case wide open. While reviewing surveillance footage from the area where the child was last seen, she noticed a figure in the background that caught her attention.

Upon closer inspection, she realized that the figure was wearing a distinctive article of clothing that had been reported missing by one of the suspects. This was the first tangible connection that they had to any of the potential suspects, and it gave Detective Girl a renewed sense of hope that they might be able to solve the case.

She immediately alerted her team, and they set out to track down the suspect who had reported the missing article of clothing. After some initial resistance, the suspect eventually agreed to come in for questioning.

Through a combination of interrogation techniques and forensic analysis, Detective Girl was able to extract valuable information from the suspect. The suspect revealed that they had been in the area at the time of the child's disappearance and had witnessed something suspicious.

With this new information, Detective Girl was able to piece together a timeline of events and narrow down the list of potential suspects. She continued to pursue leads and gather evidence, and eventually, she was able to identify the culprit responsible for the child's disappearance.

Thanks to her persistence and resourcefulness, Detective Girl was able to bring the missing child home safely and solve the case. The discovery of the new clue was a pivotal moment in the investigation and helped to turn the tide in their favor. It was a testament to Detective Girl's skills as a detective and her unwavering commitment to the case.

As Detective Girl and her team worked on the case, they faced many challenges and setbacks. They had to deal with uncooperative witnesses, misleading information, and dead-end leads. However, Detective Girl remained determined and focused on finding the missing child.

The discovery of the new clue was a breakthrough for Detective Girl and her team. It gave them a new lead to pursue and helped them to build a stronger case against the suspect. With this information, they were able to gain valuable insight into the suspect's movements and behavior around the time of the disappearance.

Through careful analysis of the evidence and interviews with potential witnesses, Detective Girl was able to piece together a timeline of events leading up to the child's disappearance. This helped her to identify the likely suspects and develop a strategy for bringing them to justice.

The pursuit of the suspects was not without its challenges, however. Detective Girl and her team had to navigate a web of lies and deception as they worked to uncover the truth. They had to be careful not to tip off the suspects or reveal their hand too soon.

Despite these challenges, Detective Girl remained focused on her goal. She continued to work tirelessly on the case, following up on leads and gathering evidence. Her hard work and determination paid off in the end, as she was able to bring the missing child home safely and solve the case.

The discovery of the new clue was a turning point in the investigation, and it helped to change the course of the case. Without it, Detective Girl and her team may never have been able to solve the case and bring the missing child home. It was a testament to her skills as a detective and her unwavering commitment to justice.

Excited by the new lead, Detective Girl and her team sprang into action, eager to investigate it further. They knew that they had to act fast if they were to find the missing child and bring them home safely.

First, they re-interviewed all the witnesses who had provided information related to the lead. They wanted to make sure that they had not missed any details the first time around. They also wanted to see if any of the witnesses had remembered anything new that could help their investigation.

Next, they turned their attention to the physical evidence. They combed through every piece of evidence they had collected so far and looked for anything that might be related to the lead. They were meticulous in their approach, leaving no stone unturned.

Through their investigation, they discovered a new piece of evidence that was crucial to the case. It was a video recording from a security camera that showed a person of interest near the location where the child was last seen. The footage was grainy and hard to make out, but Detective Girl was convinced that it was the key to solving the case.

With this new information, Detective Girl and her team began to piece together a profile of the person of interest. They looked at their movements and behavior in the days leading up to the disappearance, trying to understand their motives and their potential involvement in the case.

As they continued to investigate the lead, they faced several challenges. They encountered roadblocks and dead ends, and there were moments when it seemed like the case would never be solved. But Detective Girl remained focused and determined, determined to find the missing child and bring them home safely.

Finally, after weeks of investigation, Detective Girl and her team were able to identify the person of interest and bring them in for questioning. Through a series of interviews and interrogations, they were able to gather enough evidence to charge the suspect with kidnapping and other related crimes.

Thanks to Detective Girl's dedication and hard work, the missing child was finally found and reunited with their family. It was a victory for justice, and a testament to the power of determination and persistence in the face of adversity.

Detective Girl was relieved that the case was finally solved, but she knew that there was still work to be done. She wanted to ensure that the suspect was brought to justice and that the child's family received the support they needed to recover from the trauma.

In the aftermath of the case, Detective Girl worked closely with the prosecutor to build a strong case against the suspect. She provided testimony and evidence to support the charges, and she was present at the trial to ensure that justice was served.

At the same time, Detective Girl reached out to the child's family to offer her support and assistance. She helped them navigate the legal process and connected them with resources to help them heal from the trauma of the kidnapping. She made sure that they knew they were not alone, and that she was committed to seeing the case through to the end.

Through her efforts, Detective Girl not only solved the case, but she also helped to rebuild a shattered community. She showed that even in the darkest of times, there is hope and light to be found. And she proved that with determination, hard work, and a little bit of luck, anything is possible.

After interviewing witnesses and pursuing leads, Detective Girl began to piece together a theory of what might have happened to the missing child. She sat down with her team and went over the evidence they had gathered, trying to find any connections or patterns that might help them solve the case.

One of the first things Detective Girl noticed was that the child had been seen with a stranger just before she disappeared. The stranger had been described as a man in his thirties, with dark hair and a beard. Detective Girl suspected that this man might have been involved in the child's disappearance, but she had to find more evidence to support her theory.

As she continued to investigate, Detective Girl discovered that the child had been having trouble at school. She had been bullied by some of her classmates, and had even reported the incidents to her teacher. Detective Girl wondered if the bullying might be connected to the child's disappearance in some way.

She also learned that the child's parents had recently gone through a divorce, and that the child had been struggling with the changes in her family life. Detective Girl wondered if the stress of the divorce might have made the child more vulnerable to abduction.

Finally, Detective Girl uncovered evidence that the man seen with the child had been involved in several similar kidnappings in the past. She realized that they were dealing with a serial kidnapper, and that they needed to act fast to catch him before he could strike again.

With this new information, Detective Girl and her team began to put together a plan to catch the kidnapper and rescue the missing child. They knew that time was running out, and that they had to act quickly if they wanted to save the child's life.

As Detective Girl continued to investigate, she faced many obstacles and challenges. She encountered witnesses who were reluctant to talk, and suspects who were skilled at covering their tracks. But she persisted, using her intuition and sharp deductive skills to uncover clues and evidence.

She also had to deal with the emotional toll of the case. As a mother herself, Detective Girl felt a deep sense of responsibility to find the missing child and bring her home safely. She knew that the child's family was counting on her, and that the clock was ticking.

Despite these challenges, Detective Girl remained focused on the task at hand. She worked tirelessly to piece together the evidence and build a case against the kidnapper. And eventually, her hard work paid off.

With the help of her team, Detective Girl was able to track down the kidnapper and rescue the missing child. The child was unharmed, and her family was overjoyed to have her back home.

As the case came to a close, Detective Girl felt a sense of satisfaction and relief. She knew that there would be more cases to solve in the future, but for now, she was grateful to have helped bring this one to a successful conclusion. And she knew that the missing child case would always hold a special place in her heart, as the case that first tested her skills as a detective and showed her the true meaning of justice.

A BREAK IN THE CASE

Detective Girl had been tirelessly pursuing leads and tracking down potential suspects, but so far, all of her efforts had turned up empty. It seemed like the case of the missing child was at a dead end, and Detective Girl was starting to lose hope.

But then, one day, she received a major breakthrough. A witness had come forward with information that could crack the case wide open. The witness claimed to have seen a suspicious vehicle in the area around the time the child went missing, and had even taken down the license plate number.

Detective Girl sprang into action, using her connections in law enforcement to track down the owner of the vehicle. She discovered that the owner had a criminal record and was known to have ties to a local gang. It was starting to look like Detective Girl had found her suspect.

She and her team worked around the clock, conducting interviews and gathering evidence. They combed through surveillance footage and forensic data, looking for any clues that could connect the suspect to the crime. And finally, after days of painstaking work, they had enough evidence to make an arrest.

Detective Girl felt a surge of adrenaline as she led the team to apprehend the suspect. She knew that this was the moment she had been waiting for, the moment when justice would finally be served for the missing child and her family.

The suspect was brought in for questioning, and under intense interrogation, he eventually confessed to the crime. Detective Girl felt a mix of relief and anger as she listened to his admission. Relief that the case had finally been solved, and that the missing child had been found. But anger at the senseless and cruel act that had been committed.

In the end, though, Detective Girl knew that justice had been served. The suspect was put behind bars, and the missing child was reunited with her family. It was a bittersweet victory, but one that Detective Girl would never forget.

After the suspect was arrested and charged with the crime, Detective Girl felt a sense of closure. But there were still loose ends to tie up. She worked closely with the prosecution team to ensure that the case against the suspect was airtight, and that justice would be served.

Meanwhile, she also spent time with the family of the missing child, offering them support and updates on the progress of the investigation. She knew that the ordeal had been traumatic for them, and wanted to do everything she could to help them through it.

As the trial approached, Detective Girl prepared to testify as a witness. She had spent countless hours gathering evidence and interviewing witnesses, and was confident that her testimony would help to secure a conviction.

When the trial finally began, Detective Girl sat in the courtroom, watching as the suspect was brought before the judge. She listened as the evidence against him was presented, and watched as the prosecution team made their case.

In the end, the suspect was found guilty and sentenced to life in prison. Detective Girl felt a sense of satisfaction, knowing that justice had been served. But she also felt a sense of sadness, knowing that the family of the missing child would never fully recover from their loss.

As she left the courtroom, Detective Girl knew that this case would stay with her for a long time. It had been one of the most challenging cases she had ever worked on, and had taken a toll on her both emotionally and physically. But she also knew that she had done everything she could to bring the missing child home, and that was a source of pride for her.

In the end, Detective Girl emerged from the case a stronger and more determined detective. She knew that there would be more cases like this in the future, but she was ready for them. She was a detective, after all, and solving cases was what she did best.

Detective Girl had been working tirelessly on the missing child case for weeks, following leads, interviewing witnesses, and searching for clues. She had developed a theory about what might have happened to the child, but she needed evidence to back it up.

One day, while going through some surveillance footage from the area where the child had gone missing, Detective Girl spotted something that caught her eye. In the video, she saw a figure that looked suspicious, lurking around the area where the child had been last seen.

She immediately focused her attention on this person, digging deeper into their background and history. She discovered that they had a criminal record and had been in the area around the time of the child's disappearance. This was the break she had been looking for.

Detective Girl coordinated with her team to gather more evidence, including fingerprints and DNA samples. They scoured the area where the figure had been seen, looking for any other clues that could tie them to the disappearance.

Finally, they found it. A piece of clothing that belonged to the child was found near the location where the suspicious figure had been spotted. The clothing had traces of the suspect's DNA on it, confirming Detective Girl's theory.

With this evidence, Detective Girl was able to obtain a search warrant for the suspect's home. When they searched it, they found more evidence linking them to the disappearance of the child, including the child's belongings and other items that had been stolen from the area.

Detective Girl knew that they had enough evidence to make an arrest. She coordinated with local law enforcement to apprehend the suspect, who was taken into custody without incident.

With the evidence in hand, Detective Girl was able to piece together what had happened to the missing child. It was a heartbreaking story, but one that needed to be told. Thanks to her dedication and hard work, the family of the missing child could finally have closure and justice could be served.

Detective Girl spends hours combing through the evidence she has collected over the course of the investigation. She has a nagging feeling that there is a piece of the puzzle she is missing, but she can't quite put her finger on it.

As she is reviewing the case file once again, she notices a detail she had previously overlooked. It is a small piece of evidence, but it could be the missing link she has been searching for. She decides to follow up on this lead immediately.

She spends the next few days digging deeper into this new piece of evidence. She contacts a few more witnesses and speaks to some of the potential suspects once again. Slowly but surely, she starts to piece together a theory of what happened to the missing child.

Finally, she uncovers a piece of evidence that confirms her theory beyond a shadow of a doubt. It is a breakthrough in the case, and Detective Girl can feel the adrenaline pumping through her veins as she realizes that she may finally have the answers she has been seeking.

With her theory confirmed, Detective Girl knows that time is of the essence. She races against the clock to find the missing child before it's too late.

She shares her findings with the rest of the investigative team and they all work together to track down the suspect. They follow every lead and leave no stone unturned.

As they close in on the suspect, Detective Girl can feel her heart racing. She knows that if they don't find the missing child soon, it may be too late. She pushes herself harder than ever before, determined to bring the child home safely.

Finally, after what seems like an eternity, they locate the missing child. She is safe and unharmed, but shaken by the ordeal. Detective Girl breathes a sigh of relief as she reunites the child with their family.

She knows that this case will stay with her for a long time, but she is glad to have been a part of bringing a happy ending to such a tragic situation. She vows to continue working hard to protect and serve her community, no matter what challenges may come her way.

The moment Detective Girl sees the child, she realizes the gravity of the situation. The child is visibly traumatized and clinging to her tightly. As she comforts the child, she assures her that she is safe now and they will take her home.

The team calls for an ambulance to ensure that the child receives medical attention and a thorough check-up. Detective Girl stays with the child until the ambulance arrives, comforting her and reassuring her that everything will be okay.

After the child is taken to the hospital, Detective Girl begins the process of collecting evidence against the suspect. She knows that they need to build a strong case in order to ensure that justice is served.

Over the next few weeks, Detective Girl works tirelessly to gather all the evidence they need to prosecute the suspect. She spends long hours in the office poring over reports, interviewing witnesses, and analyzing data.

Finally, the day of the trial arrives. Detective Girl takes the stand and presents her case with confidence and conviction. Her hard work pays off as the suspect is found guilty and sentenced to a long prison term.

As she reflects on the case, Detective Girl feels a sense of pride and satisfaction. She knows that her hard work helped to bring justice to the family and closure to the community.

The case may be closed, but Detective Girl knows that there will always be new challenges and cases to tackle. She is ready and willing to face them head-on, armed with the skills, knowledge, and determination needed to protect and serve her community.

A RESCUE MISSION

As Detective Girl followed up on her leads, she found evidence that pointed her in the direction of a rundown warehouse on the outskirts of town. She knew that time was running out and she had to act fast, so she rallied her team of officers and set out on a rescue mission to find the missing child.

As they arrived at the warehouse, they noticed that it was heavily guarded, but Detective Girl knew that she had to push forward. She formulated a plan and led her team through the dark and desolate building, searching for any sign of the missing child.

The warehouse was vast and full of dangerous obstacles, but Detective Girl was determined to find the missing child. She scoured every room and corner until finally, she heard a faint cry coming from a locked storage room.

Without hesitation, Detective Girl kicked open the door and rushed inside, where she found the missing child, scared and alone. She quickly scooped up the child and carried them out of the warehouse, to the safety of waiting paramedics and family members.

With the child safely rescued, Detective Girl breathed a sigh of relief. Her hard work and determination had paid off, and she had solved the case that had been weighing heavily on her mind for weeks.

As Detective Girl held the missing child in her arms, she felt a rush of emotions wash over her. She was relieved that the child was safe, but she also felt a sense of anger and frustration at the people who had taken the child and put them in danger.

Despite her success, Detective Girl knew that the case was not yet closed. She still had to bring the culprits to justice and ensure that they would never harm another child again. She gathered her team and began the process of collecting evidence and interviewing witnesses to piece together the full story.

As the investigation continued, Detective Girl uncovered a larger criminal organization that had been operating in the city, kidnapping and trafficking children for their own gain. She worked tirelessly to bring these criminals to justice, even going undercover to gather evidence and get a firsthand look at their operations.

In the end, Detective Girl was able to dismantle the criminal organization and put the perpetrators behind bars. The missing child case had turned into a much larger operation, but thanks to Detective Girl's determination and skill, justice was served.

The experience left a lasting impact on Detective Girl, who became even more passionate about protecting children and fighting against those who would harm them. She continued to work tirelessly to solve cases and bring justice to victims, always striving to make the world a safer place for children.

As Detective Girl sets out on a rescue mission to find the missing child, she is faced with several challenges and obstacles along the way. She knows that time is running out, and the child's life may be in danger.

- Detective Girl encounters a dangerous storm, which makes it difficult for her to navigate through the city streets. She knows that the storm will make it harder for her to find the missing child, but she continues on regardless.
- While on her way to the location where the child is believed to be held, Detective Girl's car breaks down, leaving her stranded. She must rely on her wits and resourcefulness to continue the search on foot.
- As she nears the location where the child is believed to be held, Detective Girl encounters a group of hostile individuals who attempt to prevent her from continuing on her mission. She must use her self-defense skills and quick thinking to overcome the obstacles and continue on her quest to rescue the missing child.

Despite these challenges, Detective Girl perseveres and continues on her mission to rescue the missing child. She knows that failure is not an option, and she will do everything in her power to bring the child home safely.

As Detective Girl sets out on her rescue mission, she faces many obstacles and dangers that threaten her progress. Some of the challenges she encounters include:

1. Hostile Suspects: Detective Girl confronts suspects who are hostile and unwilling to cooperate with her investigation. Some of them may try to harm her or prevent her from accessing crucial information.

2.   Time Pressure: The clock is ticking, and Detective Girl has limited time to find the missing child. She has to work quickly and efficiently to gather clues and follow up on leads that could help her find the child.

3.   Environmental Hazards: The location where the child is believed to be held might be hazardous, making the rescue mission more challenging. Detective Girl has to navigate through difficult terrain, bad weather, or other environmental factors that could hinder her progress.

4.   Physical Threats: During her mission, Detective Girl may face physical threats from dangerous criminals or other unknown dangers. She has to remain alert and ready to defend herself at all times.

5.   Emotional Stress: The mission to rescue a missing child can be emotionally draining for Detective Girl. She has to remain focused and composed, even as she faces the high stakes and pressure of the situation.

Despite the obstacles she faces, Detective Girl remains committed to her mission to find the missing child and bring them home safely.

Detective Girl knew that time was running out, and every second counted. She had to act fast and think even faster if she was going to find the missing child before it was too late. With adrenaline pumping through her veins, she set out on a rescue mission, determined to bring the child home safely.

As she navigated through the dark and dangerous streets, Detective Girl encountered numerous obstacles that threatened to derail her mission. But she remained focused and resourceful, using her skills and instincts to overcome each challenge that came her way.

At one point, she found herself in a rundown warehouse, surrounded by a group of dangerous individuals who seemed determined to stop her from finding the missing child. But Detective Girl didn't back down. Instead, she used her quick thinking and martial arts skills to fend off her attackers and continue on her mission.

She also used her knowledge of the city's streets and alleys to her advantage, taking shortcuts and avoiding the heavily trafficked areas that could slow her down. With every step she took, she felt closer to the missing child, and her determination to bring the child back to safety grew stronger.

Finally, after what felt like an eternity, Detective Girl arrived at the location where she believed the missing child was being held. With caution, she approached the building, ready for whatever lay ahead.

As she made her way inside, she could hear the sound of a child's cries echoing through the halls. With renewed urgency, she raced towards the sound, determined to save the child and bring them home.

When she finally found the child, Detective Girl's heart swelled with relief and joy. With gentle hands, she scooped up the child and held them close, reassuring them that they were safe now.

Together, Detective Girl and the child made their way back to the family who had been waiting anxiously for news. As they reunited, Detective Girl felt a sense of pride and satisfaction in knowing that she had used her wits and resourcefulness to save the day and bring a missing child back to their family.

As Detective Girl rushes to find the missing child, she encounters several obstacles that threaten to derail her mission. She knows she must remain focused and think on her feet to navigate the dangerous situation and save the child.

- She assesses the situation and formulates a plan of action to get closer to the child without being detected by the kidnapper or their associates.
- Detective Girl uses her training and experience to gather information about the location and possible hiding places, trying to predict the kidnapper's next move.

- As she moves closer to the child, she uses all her wits and resourcefulness to remain undetected and to neutralize any threats that come her way.

As she approaches the location where the child is being held, she knows that the next few moments will be critical. She takes a deep breath and mentally prepares herself for the rescue mission ahead.

REUNITING THE FAMILY

After a long and perilous journey, Detective Girl finally finds the missing child. The child is scared and disoriented, but Detective Girl knows exactly what to do. She speaks to the child in a calm and reassuring voice, telling them that they are safe now and that everything will be okay.

Detective Girl takes the child by the hand and leads them out of the dangerous situation they were in. The child is weak and tired, but Detective Girl is strong and determined. She carries the child on her back and walks for miles until they reach a safe location.

As they walk, Detective Girl talks to the child and tries to distract them from their fear. She asks them about their favorite toys and games, and tells them stories about her own childhood. By the time they reach their destination, the child is feeling much better.

Detective Girl hands the child over to their grateful and emotional family. She watches as they embrace each other, tears of relief streaming down their faces. She feels a sense of pride and satisfaction in knowing that she was able to bring this family back together.

After making sure that the child is safe and sound, Detective Girl takes her leave. She walks away from the scene with a sense of accomplishment and a renewed commitment to helping those in need. She knows that there will be more cases like this one in the future, but she is ready and willing to face them head-on.

As Detective Girl arrives at the location where she believes the child is being held, she cautiously approaches the building, aware of the danger that may be waiting for her inside. She takes a deep breath, steeling herself for what may lie ahead, and pushes the door open.

The interior is dark and silent, but she can hear the sound of a child's whimpering coming from somewhere within the building. She pulls out her flashlight and begins to search the area, carefully navigating through the maze of corridors and rooms.

As she turns a corner, she spots movement out of the corner of her eye. She whips around and sees a figure darting into a nearby room. She approaches the room cautiously, her heart pounding in her chest, and slowly pushes the door open.

Inside, she finds the missing child, huddled in a corner, terrified and shaking. Detective Girl immediately rushes to the child's side, reassuring them that they are safe now and she is here to take them home.

As she helps the child to her feet, she can feel a wave of relief wash over her. After all the twists and turns of the investigation, she has finally found the missing child and brought them back to their family.

She leads the child out of the building and into the waiting arms of their parents, who are overjoyed to be reunited with their beloved child. As Detective Girl watches the happy family embrace, she can't help but feel a sense of pride in what she has accomplished.

The case may have been long and challenging, but she never gave up, and in the end, her perseverance paid off. She smiles to herself, knowing that she has truly made a difference in the lives of those she has helped.

As Detective Girl brings the missing child back to their family, emotions run high. The family members are overwhelmed with relief and gratitude, but also with fear and worry for the trauma that the child may have experienced. In this chapter, we see how Detective Girl helps the family through this difficult time and brings some closure to the case.

- The family's reaction: As Detective Girl walks into the room with the missing child, the family members erupt into a flurry of emotions. The parents are crying tears of joy, hugging their child tightly and thanking Detective Girl. The siblings are jumping up and down, laughing and crying at the same time. Detective Girl is moved by the family's reactions and feels a sense of pride in her work.
- The child's state: As the family calms down, Detective Girl takes a closer look at the child. The child is clearly traumatized and scared. They are quiet and withdrawn, avoiding eye contact with anyone. Detective Girl assures the family that the child will need professional help to cope with their experiences and provides them with resources to seek help.

- Detective Girl's reassurance: Detective Girl spends time with the family, listening to their questions and concerns. She reassures them that she will continue to work on the case and gather more information about what happened to the child. She tells them that they can count on her to support them through the legal process and any other difficulties that may arise. The family is grateful for her words of comfort and support.

The family was waiting anxiously at the police station when Detective Girl walked in with the missing child. They couldn't believe their eyes and rushed to embrace their beloved child. Detective Girl watched the scene with a sense of satisfaction and relief. She had found the missing child, and the family was finally reunited.

Here are some more details that could be added to this chapter:

- The parents cried tears of joy as they hugged their child, who looked scared but relieved to see them.
- The child's siblings were also present, and they were overjoyed to see their brother/sister again.
- Detective Girl watched the scene from a distance, feeling a sense of satisfaction and pride in her work. She had done everything she could to find the missing child and bring them back safely.
- The family thanked Detective Girl profusely, and the parents hugged her with tears in their eyes. They could never repay her for what she had done, but they promised to be forever grateful.
- Detective Girl felt emotional as well, seeing the happy ending to the case she had worked so hard on. She felt a sense of fulfillment knowing that her work had made a difference in the lives of this family.

As the chapter ends, Detective Girl is hailed as a hero by the family and the community. But she knows that her work is never truly done, as there will always be more cases to solve and people to help.

As Detective Girl watches the family embrace their missing child, she can't help but feel a sense of satisfaction knowing that she played a vital role in reuniting them. As she drives back to the station, she reflects on the case and the lessons she's learned.

• Detective Girl realizes the importance of empathy and compassion in her work as a detective.

• She recognizes the value of thoroughness and persistence in solving cases.

• She learns that no matter how challenging the case, she can always find a way to succeed with the help of her team and her own determination.

As she makes her way back to the station, she feels a sense of pride in what she has accomplished. Despite the obstacles and challenges that came her way, she never gave up and remained focused on finding the missing child.

With this case behind her, Detective Girl knows that there will always be new challenges and mysteries to solve, but she is ready for whatever comes her way. She drives into the night, ready to face whatever the future holds.

As Detective Girl sits in her office, she can't help but reflect on the case of the missing child. She thinks about the ups and downs, the twists and turns, and the emotional rollercoaster that she and the family went through. Here are some of her thoughts:

• The importance of following every lead: Detective Girl knows that sometimes, a seemingly insignificant lead can turn into a major breakthrough. She learned to always follow up on any information, no matter how small it may seem.

• The emotional toll of missing child cases: Detective Girl had worked on cases involving missing children before, but this one hit her especially hard. She realized how difficult it is

for the families involved, and the toll it can take on the investigators as well.
- The satisfaction of a job well done: Despite the challenges she faced, Detective Girl was ultimately able to find the missing child and bring them back to their family. She felt a sense of pride and satisfaction knowing that her hard work had paid off and made a difference in someone's life.
- The importance of relying on a support system: Throughout the case, Detective Girl relied on her colleagues and loved ones for emotional support. She learned that it's okay to ask for help when you need it, and that having a strong support system can make all the difference in difficult times.
- The never-ending quest for justice: Even though the case has been solved and the missing child has been found, Detective Girl knows that there are still countless other cases out there waiting to be solved. She is reminded that her work as a detective is never truly done, and that there will always be more people in need of justice and protection.

As she finishes her reflections, Detective Girl feels a sense of gratitude for the opportunity to do the work she loves and make a positive impact in people's lives. She knows that there will be more challenges and cases ahead, but she feels confident and ready to take them on.

CELEBRATING THE VICTORY

As Detective Girl brings the missing child back to their family, she is greeted with tears and hugs of gratitude. The family expresses their immense appreciation and praise for her bravery and hard work in finding their child. The news of the rescue spreads quickly, and Detective Girl's colleagues and the media alike begin to take notice.

Soon after, Detective Girl is invited to a press conference where the chief of police praises her efforts and publicly recognizes her hard work and bravery. He goes on to say that Detective Girl's dedication and resourcefulness in the case have been an inspiration to the entire police department and the community.

Detective Girl is humbled by the recognition and grateful for the opportunity to serve her community. She takes the opportunity to express her appreciation for the support she received from her colleagues and the family of the missing child throughout the case. She also reflects on the lessons she learned during the investigation and how she plans to apply them in future cases.

After the press conference, Detective Girl returns to the police station where she is greeted with high-fives and congratulations from her colleagues. They express their admiration for her work and praise her for being a role model to young detectives in the department.

As the excitement dies down, Detective Girl is left feeling both proud of her accomplishments and humbled by the responsibility that comes with being a detective. She knows that her work is never done, and she looks forward to the challenges and opportunities that lie ahead.

Detective Girl stood in front of the chief of police's desk, her heart pounding with anticipation. She had just returned from the successful rescue of the missing child, and she was eager to hear what her superiors had to say about her work.

The chief looked up from his paperwork and gave her a nod. "Detective Girl, I want to commend you on your excellent work on this case. You demonstrated great courage and resourcefulness in your efforts to find the missing child and bring them home safely."

Detective Girl felt a wave of relief wash over her. She had been anxious to hear the chief's assessment of her work, and she was thrilled to hear that he was pleased with her efforts.

"I'm just glad we were able to find the child before it was too late," she said.

The chief nodded in agreement. "Indeed. But don't downplay your role in the success of this mission. Your hard work and dedication were instrumental in bringing this child back to their family."

Detective Girl smiled, feeling a sense of pride welling up inside her. She had always known that she wanted to be a detective, and it was moments like this that made all the hard work and long hours worth it.

"Thank you, sir," she said. "I appreciate your kind words."

The chief stood up and extended his hand. "Congratulations, Detective Girl. You've earned it."

As she left the chief's office, Detective Girl couldn't help but feel a sense of satisfaction. She knew that there would always be more cases to solve, more missing children to find, but in that moment, she felt like she had made a difference in the world, one case at a time.

As news of the safe return of the missing child spread throughout the community, people began to celebrate. The local news channels covered the story extensively, and Detective Girl was hailed as a hero.

The family of the missing child held a press conference, where they thanked Detective Girl and the police department for their hard work and dedication to finding their child. They expressed their immense gratitude and relief that their child was home safe.

The community came together to throw a celebration in honor of the missing child's safe return. There were balloons, music, and plenty of food for everyone to enjoy. Detective Girl attended the celebration, and she was met with cheers and applause from the crowd.

As she looked around at the smiling faces of the community members, Detective Girl couldn't help but feel a sense of pride and satisfaction. She had been able to bring a missing child home to their family, and that was an accomplishment she would always be proud of.

The police department also recognized Detective Girl's hard work and dedication by awarding her with a medal of honor. She was humbled and grateful to receive such a prestigious award.

In the weeks following the case, Detective Girl continued to receive messages of thanks and praise from members of the community. She knew that she had made a difference, and that was all the recognition she needed.

Although the case had been emotionally and physically draining, Detective Girl had learned a lot from it. She had learned the importance of perseverance, teamwork, and trusting her instincts. She knew that these lessons would serve her well in her future cases as a detective.

As the celebration came to an end, Detective Girl couldn't help but feel grateful for the community's support and for the opportunity to bring a missing child home. She knew that it was moments like these that made all the hard work and long hours worth it.

Detective Girl was greeted with cheers and applause as she made her way through the streets, the missing child safely in her arms. It was a beautiful day, the sun shining down on the town square where a small crowd had gathered to welcome them back.

The child's family rushed forward, tears streaming down their faces as they embraced their loved one. Detective Girl stepped back, giving them a moment to reunite before she was surrounded by the grateful townspeople.

"Thank you, Detective Girl," one woman exclaimed, hugging her tightly. "We were all so worried about the little one."

Others echoed her sentiments, shaking her hand, patting her back, and offering words of praise and admiration. Detective Girl smiled graciously, accepting their gratitude but never forgetting that it was the teamwork and perseverance of everyone involved that made this happy ending possible.

As the celebration continued, Detective Girl couldn't help but reflect on the case and the lessons she had learned. She realized that every case was unique, and that each required a careful and thoughtful approach. She had learned to listen to her instincts, to follow her leads wherever they may take her, and to never give up hope.

But most importantly, she had learned the value of working together with others. From the witnesses and suspects she had interviewed to the officers who had assisted her in the search, it had been a group effort that ultimately led to the safe return of the missing child.

Detective Girl knew that there would be more cases to come, and that each one would present its own set of challenges. But as she looked around at the smiling faces of the community, she felt a renewed sense of purpose and determination. She was ready to face whatever lay ahead, knowing that she had the support of those around her and the knowledge that she had made a difference in someone's life.

Detective Girl was honored for her dedication and hard work in bringing the missing child back home safely. The community came together to show their appreciation for her service and bravery.

At a ceremony held in her honor, Detective Girl was awarded a medal of honor by the mayor for her exceptional efforts in solving the case. She stood on stage, proud and humbled by the recognition she was receiving.

As she looked out into the crowd, she saw the grateful faces of the child's family, who couldn't thank her enough for bringing their loved one back home. She also saw the faces of many members of the community, who had come out to support her and to show their appreciation for the work that she had done. Detective Girl was touched by the outpouring of love and support from the community. She knew that it wasn't just about her, but about all of the people who had come together to bring the child home safely.

In her acceptance speech, Detective Girl thanked everyone who had helped her along the way, from the witnesses and potential suspects she had interviewed to the officers who had supported her throughout the investigation. She also thanked the child's family for their trust and for allowing her to be a part of bringing their loved one back home.

As the ceremony came to a close, Detective Girl felt a sense of pride and accomplishment. She had worked hard to solve the case and had put her heart and soul into bringing the missing child home safely. And now, as the community celebrated together, she knew that her hard work had truly paid off.

Detective Girl was thrilled to receive recognition for her hard work in finding the missing child. She was honored by the community and her colleagues, who praised her for her dedication and bravery. The chief of police even gave her a commendation for her outstanding work.

The media was also eager to interview Detective Girl, and she found herself in the spotlight for a few days. She gave several interviews in which she talked about the case and the importance of finding missing children. She also gave advice to parents and guardians on how to keep their children safe.

Despite all the attention, Detective Girl remained humble and focused on the case. She knew that she had done her job, but she also knew that there were still many other missing children out there who needed to be found.

After the case was closed, Detective Girl took some time off to rest and recharge. She spent time with her family and friends, and enjoyed some well-deserved downtime. But she knew that she would soon be back at work, tackling new cases and helping to keep her community safe.

As she reflected on the case, Detective Girl realized that she had learned a lot about herself and her abilities as a detective. She had faced numerous challenges and obstacles along the way, but she had always persevered and remained focused on her goal. She also realized how important it was to work as a team and to rely on the support of her colleagues.

The experience had made Detective Girl more determined than ever to continue her work as a detective. She knew that there were still many more children out there who needed her help, and she was ready to do whatever it took to find them.

BACK TO REALITY

After the intense and emotional case of the missing child, Detective Girl returns to her everyday life. She takes some time off to recover from the physically and mentally exhausting work she had been doing for the past few weeks. She spends her days resting, catching up with friends and family, and doing activities that she enjoys.

As she slowly transitions back into work mode, she begins to work on smaller cases and tasks. The contrast between the high-pressure case she had just wrapped up and these smaller tasks is a welcome change of pace. She finds joy in the simplicity of some of the cases and the feeling of closure she is able to provide to those she helps.

As the weeks go by, the memory of the missing child case still lingers in her mind. She reflects on the lessons she learned during that time and the ways in which it changed her perspective on life. She realizes the importance of cherishing the time we have with our loved ones and being grateful for every moment we have.

Detective Girl also begins to appreciate the support she received from her colleagues and the community during the case. She recognizes that it takes a village to solve complex cases and is grateful for the team effort that went into finding the missing child.

Overall, Detective Girl returns to her everyday life with a renewed sense of purpose and gratitude. She continues to serve her community with dedication and passion, knowing that every case is an opportunity to make a difference in someone's life.

Detective Girl returned to her everyday life after the intense case that consumed her for weeks. She felt a mix of emotions - relief, satisfaction, and exhaustion. She took a few days off work to rest and spend time with her loved ones. She also used this time to reflect on the case and the lessons she learned.

During her reflection, Detective Girl realized that the case reminded her of the importance of persistence and never giving up. Even when it seemed like there was no hope, she continued to push forward, gathering clues and following leads until she cracked the case.

She also thought about the importance of teamwork. Detective Girl had received help from her colleagues, witnesses, and community members, all of whom played a crucial role in solving the case. She knew that it was only by working together that they were able to bring the missing child back home.

As Detective Girl returned to work, she felt renewed and energized. She was eager to continue serving her community and helping those in need. She knew that there were always going to be more cases that needed solving, and she was ready to tackle them head-on.

But for now, she was happy to be back at her desk, sifting through case files and working on new leads. She knew that her next case could come at any moment, and she was ready for whatever challenges it might bring.

After successfully solving the case and reuniting the missing child with their family, Detective Girl returned to her everyday life. However, she found it hard to shake off the trauma of the case. She struggled to adjust to the aftermath of the case, as memories of the investigation continued to haunt her.

Despite her best efforts to move on, Detective Girl found herself constantly thinking about the case. She replayed the events in her mind, second-guessing her decisions and wondering if there was anything she could have done differently. She found it hard to sleep, plagued by nightmares of the missing child and the dangers she faced while on the rescue mission.

Detective Girl tried to distract herself by immersing herself in other cases and her personal life. She spent more time with her family and friends, trying to create happy memories to replace the darker ones from the case. She also took on new cases, hoping that the fresh challenges would help her to move on.

However, nothing seemed to work. Detective Girl realized that she needed help to process the trauma of the case. She sought out a therapist and began attending regular sessions. With the help of the therapist, she learned to confront her feelings and process the trauma in a healthy way.

It wasn't easy, but slowly, Detective Girl began to find peace. She learned to accept that there were some things she couldn't control, and that it was okay to ask for help. She also learned to appreciate the positive impact she had on the community by solving the case and bringing the missing child home.

Over time, Detective Girl was able to let go of the trauma of the case and return to her work with a renewed sense of purpose. She continued to solve cases and help the community, but now she did so with a deeper understanding of the importance of self-care and seeking help when needed.

Detective Girl struggled to adjust to the aftermath of the case. She couldn't help but replay the events of the case in her mind. She kept wondering if she could have done more to prevent the child from being abducted. She knew that the case was over, but she couldn't shake off the feeling of guilt.

The detective tried to distract herself by diving into work, but it wasn't easy. She found herself losing focus on tasks and had trouble sleeping at night. Her colleagues noticed the change in her behavior and offered to help, but she refused to open up.

One day, Detective Girl decided to take a break from work and visited a therapist. She hoped that talking about the case and her emotions would help her come to terms with what happened. During the therapy session, the detective learned that it was normal to feel guilty and helpless after such a traumatic event.

The therapist helped her process the emotions she had been suppressing and taught her healthy coping mechanisms. With the help of the therapist, the detective began to see things from a different perspective. She realized that she had done everything she could to find the missing child and that sometimes things were out of her control.

Eventually, the detective started to feel more like herself again. She returned to work with a renewed sense of purpose and a better understanding of her emotional well-being. She made sure to take care of herself by taking breaks when needed and seeking support from her colleagues.

Through this experience, Detective Girl learned that it's essential to prioritize her emotional health and not neglect it in the face of challenging cases. She knew that she would face similar situations in the future, but now she was better equipped to handle them.

Detective Girl had solved many cases before, but this one had taken a toll on her in ways she hadn't anticipated. The missing child case had been particularly difficult, and the relief she felt when they were found had been immense. However, in the days that followed, she found herself struggling with the emotional aftermath.

She would wake up in the middle of the night, her mind racing with thoughts of the case. She couldn't help but think about the child and what they must have gone through. She would replay the events of the case in her mind, wondering if there was anything more she could have done.

She tried to push the thoughts aside and focus on other things, but they would always come creeping back. She found herself withdrawing from her friends and family, feeling like she couldn't talk to them about what she was going through.

Finally, she realized that she needed to take care of herself. She made an appointment with a therapist and talked through her feelings about the case. It was difficult, but she knew it was necessary to process everything she had experienced.

She also started taking up hobbies again, trying to find ways to relax and unwind. She would take long walks in the park or spend time cooking in the kitchen. She even started practicing yoga, which helped her find a sense of calm.

As time went on, she started to feel more like herself again. The memories of the case were still there, but they didn't consume her like they had before. She knew that she would always carry the experience with her, but she was ready to move forward and continue doing the work she loved.

As Detective Girl returns to her normal routine, she finds it difficult to shake off the emotional toll the case has taken on her. She has spent countless hours working tirelessly to bring the missing child home, but now that the case is closed, she feels a sense of emptiness and fatigue. She realizes that she has neglected her personal life, and it is time to focus on herself for a while.

The memories of the case keep haunting her, and she has trouble sleeping at night. She thinks about the family of the missing child and wonders how they are coping with the aftermath of the ordeal. She feels a sense of guilt, wondering if she could have done more to bring the child home sooner.

To cope with her emotions, Detective Girl turns to therapy. She seeks the help of a professional who specializes in trauma counseling. Through therapy, she learns to process her emotions and find ways to cope with the stress and trauma of the case. She also reaches out to her colleagues who have gone through similar experiences, and they offer her support and understanding.

As time passes, Detective Girl begins to heal from the emotional wounds of the case. She takes some time off work to rest and rejuvenate. She spends time with her loved ones and focuses on her hobbies and interests. She also starts volunteering at a local shelter for children, hoping to make a positive impact in the lives of those who need it the most.

Through her struggles, Detective Girl learns the importance of self-care and the value of seeking help when needed. She also learns that it's okay to take a step back and focus on her personal life. She is proud of the work she has done in the case and is grateful for the opportunity to serve her community. She knows that she has made a difference in the lives of the missing child and their family, and that is what matters the most.

NEW CHALLENGES

Detective Girl had just wrapped up a difficult case and was taking some time off to recharge when she received a call from the police chief. There was a new case that needed her attention. A wealthy businessman had been found dead in his office, and there were no signs of forced entry.
Detective Girl accepted the case and arrived at the crime scene. She examined the body and the office for any evidence

that could provide a clue to what had happened. She also interviewed the victim's family, friends, and colleagues to get a better understanding of the victim's personal and professional life.

As she dug deeper, Detective Girl discovered that the victim had many enemies in the business world. He had made several enemies through aggressive business tactics and shady deals. She also found evidence that suggested the victim was involved in some illegal activities.

Despite the numerous suspects and the complexity of the case, Detective Girl remained focused and determined to solve it. She worked tirelessly, analyzing the evidence and following up on leads. She even put herself in harm's way to get the information she needed.

Finally, after weeks of investigation, Detective Girl pieced together the puzzle and identified the killer. It turned out that the victim's business partner had killed him because he discovered the victim was planning to turn him in for embezzlement.

Detective Girl presented her findings to the police chief, who was impressed with her work. She had once again solved a difficult case and brought justice to the victim and their family.

Despite her success, Detective Girl couldn't shake the emotional toll the case had taken on her. She took some time off to recuperate before taking on her next case, knowing that she needed to be mentally and emotionally prepared for the challenges ahead.

Detective Girl was in her office, sipping on a cup of coffee when her phone rang. She answered it and listened intently to the voice on the other end. It was the police chief, and he had a new case for her to work on.

As he briefed her on the details of the case, Detective Girl felt a rush of adrenaline. It had been a while since she had taken on a new case, and she was eager to get started. The chief gave her the address of the crime scene and instructed her to meet with the officers on duty there.

Detective Girl quickly gathered her things and headed out the door, her mind already racing with possibilities. She knew that every case was different, but she couldn't help but feel that she was ready for whatever this one might throw at her.

As she arrived at the scene of the crime, she could see the flashing lights of the police cars and the gathered crowds. She made her way through the throngs of people, flashing her badge as she went, until she reached the officers.

They filled her in on what they knew so far - a local business had been robbed, and there was evidence of forced entry. Detective Girl examined the scene carefully, taking notes and making mental calculations.

As she worked, she couldn't help but feel a sense of excitement. This was what she was trained to do, and she was good at it. She was determined to solve this case and bring the perpetrator to justice.

The hours flew by as she gathered evidence and interviewed witnesses. She could feel herself getting closer to the truth with every passing moment. Finally, she was able to piece together the clues and make a breakthrough in the case.

With renewed energy, she followed the trail of evidence, and it wasn't long before she found herself standing face to face with the suspect. The suspect tried to run, but Detective Girl was faster. She apprehended the suspect and turned them over to the police.

As the case wrapped up, Detective Girl felt a sense of satisfaction wash over her. She had done it again. She had solved another case and brought justice to the community. And with that, she knew that she was ready for whatever case came her way next.

Detective Girl was back at work, ready to take on a new case. She had just finished a difficult one, but her passion for solving mysteries and bringing justice to victims kept her motivated.

The new case was unlike any she had seen before. It involved a series of burglaries that took place in a wealthy neighborhood. The burglars were clever and left no evidence behind, making it difficult for the police to track them down.

Detective Girl was determined to crack the case, but she knew it wouldn't be easy. She gathered as much information as she could, interviewing witnesses and analyzing crime scene photos. She soon realized that the burglars were not acting alone, but were part of a larger criminal organization.

As she dug deeper, she faced new challenges and obstacles. The criminal organization was well-funded and had connections in high places, making it difficult to gather evidence and make arrests. Detective Girl knew she had to be careful and use all her resources to stay one step ahead of the criminals.

One night, as she was going through the evidence, she received a threatening message from the organization. They warned her to back off the case or face dire consequences. But Detective Girl was not one to be intimidated. She knew that backing down would only embolden the criminals and put more people at risk.

She continued to investigate, working tirelessly to gather evidence and build a case against the organization. She faced many setbacks and roadblocks, but she refused to give up. Her dedication and determination paid off when she finally uncovered the identity of the leader of the organization.

But her victory was short-lived. The leader had anticipated her move and had fled the country before the police could apprehend him. Detective Girl was disappointed, but she knew that her hard work had dealt a major blow to the organization. She was confident that they would not be able to operate as freely as before.

Despite not being able to catch the leader, Detective Girl was proud of the progress she had made. She knew that there would always be challenges and obstacles in her line of work, but she was prepared to face them head-on. She was already looking forward to her next case, ready to make a difference and bring justice to those who needed it.

Detective Girl was back to work, but the memories of the last case lingered in her mind. She had barely had time to process everything that had happened, and now she was thrown into a new case that required her full attention.

As she delved deeper into the new case, she realized that this one was going to be just as challenging as the last. She faced new obstacles and challenges that she had not encountered before, and it seemed like every lead she followed led to a dead end.

The pressure of the new case, coupled with the emotional toll of the last one, weighed heavily on her. Detective Girl found herself struggling to keep up with the demands of her job, and it was taking a toll on her physically and mentally.

She knew that she needed to take care of herself if she was going to be of any use to the case. She started taking breaks when she needed them, and made sure to take care of her physical and mental health. She talked to a therapist to help her deal with the emotional toll of the previous case.

As she began to prioritize her own well-being, Detective Girl found that she was able to approach the new case with renewed energy and focus. She was able to tackle each obstacle with a clear mind and a renewed sense of purpose.

With her newfound resilience, she was able to uncover new leads and evidence that brought her closer to solving the case. It wasn't easy, but she pushed through the challenges and obstacles with determination.

Eventually, Detective Girl was able to crack the case and bring the perpetrator to justice. Although the emotional toll of the case was still present, she was proud of the work she had done, and was glad to have brought closure to the victims and their families.

The experience taught Detective Girl an important lesson - that taking care of oneself was crucial, especially in high-stress jobs like hers. She made a promise to herself to prioritize her own well-being, even in the midst of difficult cases.

Detective Girl had been eagerly waiting for her next case. After the emotional rollercoaster of the previous case, she was eager to put her skills to the test once again. She received a call from the police department and was assigned to a new case.

The case involved a missing person, a young woman who had disappeared from her apartment two days ago. Detective Girl immediately began gathering information about the missing woman. She spoke with the woman's friends and family, scoured social media for any clues, and obtained footage from nearby surveillance cameras.

As she began to piece together the woman's last known whereabouts, she discovered that the woman had a history of substance abuse and had been struggling with addiction for some time. Detective Girl knew that this would complicate the case, as addiction can lead to erratic behavior and make it more difficult to track someone's movements.

Undeterred, Detective Girl continued to gather evidence and follow leads. She worked tirelessly, putting in long hours and sacrificing her personal life for the sake of the case. She knew that time was of the essence, and that every minute counted.

Despite her best efforts, however, Detective Girl faced a number of challenges and obstacles along the way. Witnesses were uncooperative or provided conflicting information, and there were several dead ends in the investigation. At times, Detective Girl felt as though she was hitting a wall and making no progress.

But she refused to give up. She used the skills she had learned on the previous case to approach the investigation from different angles and consider alternative scenarios. She collaborated with her colleagues and sought advice from experts in the field. And slowly but surely, she began to piece together a picture of what had happened to the missing woman.

As Detective Girl got closer to cracking the case, she also faced personal challenges. The long hours and emotional toll of the job began to take a toll on her mental health, and she struggled to balance her work and personal life. But she knew that the stakes were too high to give up now. She had to find the missing woman and bring her home to her family.

Finally, after days of relentless work and investigation, Detective Girl found the missing woman. She had been hiding out in a nearby hotel, too ashamed to face her family and friends after her latest relapse. Detective Girl was able to convince the woman to return home, and she was reunited with her loved ones.

Though the case was emotionally draining and challenging, Detective Girl was proud of the work she had done. She knew that it was cases like these that reminded her why she became a detective in the first place. And as she closed the case and moved on to the next one, she felt more determined than ever to make a difference and bring justice to those who needed it most.

As Detective Girl delves deeper into the new case, she finds herself drawing on the lessons she learned during her previous investigation. She knows that solving a case requires a combination of intelligence, creativity, and perseverance. She must remain focused on the task at hand, gathering evidence and following leads, even when it seems like a dead end.

Detective Girl has also learned that the support of her colleagues and loved ones is crucial in maintaining her mental and emotional well-being. She makes sure to lean on those she trusts when the weight of the case becomes too heavy to bear alone.

As she uncovers more information, Detective Girl realizes that this new case is more complex than she originally thought. She faces new challenges and obstacles that she has never encountered before. However, she remains determined to bring the perpetrator to justice and provide closure for the victims and their families.

Detective Girl knows that her success is not only measured by the resolution of the case but also by the relationships she builds along the way. She makes sure to communicate effectively with her team members and works collaboratively to solve the case. Her empathy and compassion for the victims and their families also enable her to build strong relationships with them, which she believes is essential in her line of work.

As the investigation progresses, Detective Girl continues to apply the lessons she has learned, making progress in the case. She knows that it may take some time to bring the perpetrator to justice, but she remains committed to seeing the case through to the end.

DISCOVERING NEW CLUES

Detective Girl had been working on the new case for several days when she finally came across a lead that seemed promising. She had been poring over witness statements and surveillance footage when she noticed something odd in one of the videos.

At first, it seemed like nothing more than a coincidence, but as she continued to study the footage, Detective Girl realized that the person in the video matched the description of a potential suspect in the case.

With renewed energy, she set out to investigate the lead further. She spoke to witnesses in the area, showing them a photo of the person in the video. Several people recognized the individual and were able to provide information on their whereabouts.

Following up on these leads, Detective Girl was able to track down the suspect and bring them in for questioning. Though the suspect initially denied any involvement in the crime, Detective Girl was able to present evidence that linked them to the scene.

Feeling a sense of satisfaction, Detective Girl continued to work on the case, determined to bring justice to the victim and their family.

Detective Girl spent countless hours investigating the new case, but she was still struggling to find any leads. However, she didn't lose hope and continued to search for any possible clues. One day, while she was going through some old records at the local police station, she came across a name that caught her attention.

The name belonged to a man who had a history of committing similar crimes in the past. Detective Girl immediately knew that she had to investigate this lead further, so she went to the man's last known address to see if he was still there.

To her surprise, the man was still living at the same address, and he was more than willing to speak with her. He claimed that he had reformed and had not committed any crimes in a long time. Detective Girl was skeptical, but she listened to what he had to say.

As she was leaving the man's house, she noticed something odd about the way his yard was arranged. She decided to investigate further and found a hidden compartment in the ground that contained some suspicious items. She knew that this was the break she had been looking for, and she took the evidence back to the lab for analysis.

The analysis revealed that the items were linked to the crime that Detective Girl was investigating. She had finally found a major clue that could help her solve the case.

Detective Girl spent the morning reviewing the new case file, pouring over every detail and trying to come up with a strategy for how to approach it. As she dug deeper into the case, she began to notice a pattern that seemed familiar. It reminded her of a case she had worked on years ago.

With this realization, Detective Girl decided to follow up on some of the leads from that old case. She reached out to her former colleagues and asked for their assistance. Together, they began to investigate the new leads, carefully scrutinizing each detail to ensure that they were on the right track.

As they delved deeper into the investigation, they began to unravel a complex web of deceit and betrayal. The case was far more intricate than they had initially thought, with numerous suspects and possible motives.

Detective Girl spent long hours pouring over evidence, questioning witnesses, and following leads. The pressure was intense, but she remained focused on the task at hand. She was determined to find the truth, no matter what it took.

Despite the obstacles and setbacks along the way, Detective Girl's diligence and persistence eventually paid off. She uncovered a critical piece of evidence that would change the course of the investigation.

With this new evidence in hand, Detective Girl and her team continued to pursue the leads until they finally uncovered the truth. It was a tense and dramatic moment, but ultimately, they were able to bring the perpetrator to justice.

As she walked away from the case, Detective Girl felt a sense of accomplishment and satisfaction. It had been a difficult and challenging investigation, but she had managed to solve it. It was a testament to her skills as a detective and her unwavering commitment to justice.

As Detective Girl continues to investigate the new case, she follows up on every lead she can find. She speaks to witnesses, reviews surveillance footage, and studies any evidence she can find.

One lead takes her to a local pawn shop, where she discovers that a suspect in the case has sold a valuable piece of jewelry recently. The pawnbroker is able to provide Detective Girl with information about the suspect, including their name and address.

Detective Girl heads to the address and conducts a search of the premises. She discovers a number of items that are of interest to the case, including a bloodstained jacket and a suspicious-looking package. She collects these items as evidence and takes them back to the station for analysis.

As she pores over the evidence, Detective Girl realizes that the blood on the jacket matches that of the victim in the case. She also finds evidence in the package that links the suspect to the crime.

With this new information, Detective Girl is able to piece together what happened and identify the suspect. She calls in backup and heads out to make the arrest.

As Detective Girl followed up on the leads, she slowly began to unravel a new mystery. The clues she had gathered led her to believe that there was more to this case than what had originally been presented to her.

She spent countless hours poring over evidence and interviewing witnesses, trying to piece together what had happened. The more she dug, the more the pieces began to fall into place, revealing a tangled web of deceit and corruption.

Detective Girl knew she had to be careful. She was getting close to the truth, but she wasn't sure who she could trust. She had a gut feeling that there were people who didn't want her to solve this case and would do anything to stop her.

Despite the danger, Detective Girl persisted, determined to uncover the truth and bring justice to the victims. She knew that the truth would be painful for some, but she believed it was necessary to expose the wrongdoings and hold those responsible accountable.

As she got closer to the truth, the pressure mounted, and the stakes became higher. She knew she had to be strategic and careful in her actions, but she couldn't let fear hold her back.

With each new discovery, Detective Girl's resolve grew stronger. She was more determined than ever to see this case through to the end, no matter the cost.

Detective Girl had been working on the new case for weeks, following up on leads, interviewing witnesses, and gathering evidence. As she dug deeper into the case, she began to uncover a web of deceit and secrets that seemed to go all the way to the top.

The case involved a wealthy businessman who had been found dead in his office under suspicious circumstances. At first, it appeared to be a straightforward case of suicide, but Detective Girl knew better. There were too many unanswered questions, too many loose ends.

She began to suspect that the businessman had been murdered, and that someone was covering it up. She followed the trail of evidence, slowly piecing together the puzzle. Along the way, she encountered many obstacles and challenges. But she was determined to see the case through to the end.

As she got closer to the truth, she began to feel a sense of unease. This case was different from any she had worked on before. The stakes were higher, the danger greater. She knew that if she didn't solve the case soon, more lives could be at risk.

But Detective Girl was not one to give up easily. She pressed on, following every lead, turning over every stone. And finally, after weeks of hard work, she discovered a piece of evidence that changed everything.

The evidence led her to the killer, a close associate of the businessman who had been embezzling money from the company for years. When confronted, the killer broke down and confessed to the crime.

It was a bittersweet victory for Detective Girl. She had solved the case, but it had taken a toll on her emotionally and physically. She couldn't help but wonder how many more cases like this were out there, waiting to be solved.

But for now, she allowed herself a moment of satisfaction. She had brought a killer to justice, and that was something to be proud of.

BUILDING A CASE

Detective Girl spent countless hours reviewing the evidence she had gathered, trying to find any patterns or connections that could lead her closer to the truth. After many long nights of poring over documents, she began to piece together the evidence and build a case.

As she reviewed each piece of evidence, a new puzzle began to emerge, and she found herself drawing connections between seemingly unrelated pieces of information. She carefully studied each detail, looking for any inconsistencies or clues that could help her solve the mystery.

Finally, after weeks of hard work, Detective Girl felt like she had a solid understanding of the case. She was confident that she had identified the key players and had a good idea of what had happened. But she knew that she needed more evidence to make her case.

She put together a team of investigators to help her gather the evidence she needed. They spent days interviewing witnesses and analyzing documents, slowly building a case that would stand up in court.

Finally, the day arrived when Detective Girl felt like she had enough evidence to make an arrest. She carefully reviewed the case with her team, going over every detail to ensure that they were ready to proceed.

With a sense of determination and purpose, Detective Girl and her team headed out to make their move. They arrived at the suspect's location, and after a tense standoff, they were able to apprehend the suspect and bring them into custody.

As Detective Girl looked at the suspect, she couldn't help but feel a sense of satisfaction. She had worked tirelessly to build this case, and now justice would be served.

But even as she celebrated her victory, she knew that her work was far from over. There were always more cases to solve, more mysteries to unravel, and more justice to be served. And Detective Girl was ready to take on whatever challenges lay ahead.

Detective Girl spent countless hours going through the evidence, analyzing every detail, and building a case. She knew that this new mystery was going to be a tough one to crack, but she was determined to see it through to the end.

As she sifted through the evidence, she began to piece together a pattern of behavior that led her to believe that the culprit was someone close to the victim. The more she dug, the more convinced she became that she was on the right track.

She spent long days and nights pouring over the details, trying to make sense of the evidence she had gathered. Finally, after weeks of hard work, she was ready to make her move.

With a solid case built, Detective Girl gathered her team and prepared to make an arrest. She knew that this was going to be a delicate situation and that she needed to be careful in how she proceeded.

With her team in place, Detective Girl moved in and made the arrest. The culprit was shocked to see Detective Girl and her team, and he knew that he had been caught.

As the suspect was taken away in handcuffs, Detective Girl felt a sense of satisfaction wash over her. She had done her job, and justice had been served. But even as she celebrated the successful conclusion of the case, she knew that there would be more work to do.

For Detective Girl, the mystery never ended. There was always another case to solve, another mystery to unravel. But she knew that with hard work, determination, and a commitment to justice, she would always be up to the task.

Detective Girl spent countless hours going over the evidence, looking for any pattern or clue that could give her insight into the case. As she sifted through the information, she began to see a possible connection between seemingly unrelated pieces of evidence.

She couldn't shake off the feeling that something wasn't quite right about the case. Every time she thought she was getting closer to the truth, something would come up that would make her rethink her theory.

But after weeks of investigation, Detective Girl finally formed a theory of what happened. She believed that the perpetrator was someone close to the victim, perhaps a family member or a close friend.

The evidence seemed to point to this theory, but she knew she needed to find concrete proof before she could make an arrest. She continued to follow up on leads and gather more evidence to support her theory.

She worked tirelessly, poring over every detail and scrutinizing every piece of evidence until she was certain that she had a solid case. Finally, she felt confident that she had enough to make an arrest and bring the perpetrator to justice.

As Detective Girl pieced together the evidence, she began to form a theory of what had happened. She spent long hours going over the facts, considering different scenarios and trying to fill in the gaps. She consulted with her colleagues and sought advice from experts in the relevant fields.

As she delved deeper into the case, Detective Girl became increasingly convinced that her theory was correct. She knew that she needed to proceed with caution, however, and make sure that she had all the evidence she needed to build a strong case.

She worked tirelessly to gather additional evidence, interviewing witnesses, re-examining crime scenes, and following up on any leads that might help her confirm her theory. Finally, after weeks of hard work and dedication, she had all the pieces she needed to build a compelling case.

With her theory firmly in place and the evidence to back it up, Detective Girl began to prepare for the next phase of the investigation. She knew that she would need to be meticulous in her preparation, anticipating every possible objection and making sure that her case was airtight.

As she worked, Detective Girl felt a sense of purpose and determination that she hadn't experienced in a long time. She knew that this case was important and that the outcome could have a significant impact on the community. She was determined to get it right, no matter what.

Finally, the day arrived when Detective Girl was ready to present her case. She stood before the judge and the jury, confident in her theory and the evidence she had gathered. As she spoke, she could see the reactions of those in the courtroom. Some were skeptical, but others were nodding their heads, convinced by her argument.

In the end, the judge and the jury agreed with Detective Girl's theory, and the accused was found guilty. It was a moment of triumph for Detective Girl, and she felt a sense of pride and satisfaction that she had rarely experienced before.

As she walked out of the courtroom, Detective Girl knew that there would be more cases to solve in the future. But for now, she allowed herself to bask in the glory of a job well done, confident in the knowledge that she had made a difference.

Detective Girl spent long hours researching and gathering information on potential suspects. She was determined to find the culprit and bring them to justice. She spent time observing their behavior, collecting physical evidence, and interviewing people who knew them.

After several weeks of investigation, Detective Girl was able to narrow down her list of potential suspects to a few individuals. She carefully analyzed their movements, habits, and known associates. She even went undercover to gain more information and gather evidence.

One evening, Detective Girl received a phone call from one of her informants. They had seen one of her potential suspects acting suspiciously near the scene of the crime. Without hesitation, Detective Girl sprang into action. She gathered her team and headed out to investigate.

As they arrived at the scene, Detective Girl spotted the suspect trying to escape. She quickly ordered her team to surround the area and gave chase. After a few tense minutes, they managed to catch up to the suspect and apprehend them.

Back at the station, Detective Girl interrogated the suspect, using all the evidence she had gathered to pressure them into confessing. After several hours of questioning, the suspect finally broke down and admitted to the crime.

Detective Girl was relieved that her hard work had paid off. She had successfully solved the case and brought the perpetrator to justice. She took a moment to reflect on the case and how she had grown as a detective. She knew that this was just the beginning of many more cases to come, but she was ready for whatever challenges lay ahead.

As Detective Girl delved deeper into the case, she began to uncover new leads and potential suspects. She spent long hours going through surveillance footage, interviewing witnesses, and analyzing forensic evidence. Each piece of evidence she collected added a new layer to the puzzle, and Detective Girl was determined to put all the pieces together.

She spent weeks following up on leads, questioning potential suspects, and gathering evidence. Slowly but surely, she began to piece together a picture of what had happened. However, each lead brought new challenges and obstacles, and Detective Girl found herself facing many setbacks.

Despite these challenges, Detective Girl remained focused and determined. She was relentless in her pursuit of the truth and refused to give up until she had solved the case. Each new discovery she made fueled her determination and pushed her to work even harder.

As the investigation progressed, Detective Girl's theory began to take shape. She began to suspect that the crime was part of a larger conspiracy and that there were more people involved than she had initially thought. She knew that the key to solving the case was to find the missing piece of the puzzle that would tie everything together.

With this in mind, Detective Girl redoubled her efforts and began to pursue her new leads with renewed vigor. She knew that time was running out, and she needed to find the missing piece of the puzzle before it was too late.

CLOSING IN

Detective Girl had been working tirelessly on the new case. She had been following leads and gathering evidence for weeks, and finally, she was beginning to piece together the puzzle.

After examining the evidence and following up on leads, she had narrowed down her list of suspects to a few individuals who had motive and opportunity to commit the crime. She knew that if she could just find the right piece of evidence, she would be able to make an arrest and solve the case.

One morning, as she was going over the evidence again, she noticed something that had previously gone unnoticed. A small detail, but one that could make all the difference in the case.

With a newfound sense of excitement, Detective Girl began to follow this new lead. She went back to interview witnesses, reviewed surveillance footage, and worked tirelessly to build a stronger case against her suspects.

As she delved deeper into the case, she discovered more and more evidence that pointed to one particular suspect. She couldn't ignore the feeling that this was the person responsible for the crime.

After gathering enough evidence, Detective Girl made the decision to move forward with an arrest warrant. She assembled a team of officers and set out to make the arrest.

The tension was high as they approached the suspect's house, but with a well-executed plan, they were able to make the arrest without incident.

Back at the station, Detective Girl and her team went through the suspect's belongings and found more evidence that confirmed their suspicions. The suspect finally confessed to the crime, and Detective Girl had successfully solved another case.

She couldn't help but feel a sense of satisfaction as she reflected on the hard work and dedication that went into solving the case. It was a reminder of why she became a detective in the first place - to bring justice to those who had been wronged.

As Detective Girl continued to investigate, she found more and more evidence that supported her theory. She followed up on leads, conducted interviews, and sifted through piles of paperwork.

After weeks of tireless work, she finally found a breakthrough. A key witness came forward with new information that shed light on the case. Detective Girl immediately knew that this could be the missing piece she needed to solve the case.

She spent countless hours analyzing the information and building a case. She worked tirelessly, often pulling all-nighters, to piece together the evidence and make sure everything was airtight.

Finally, after what felt like an eternity, Detective Girl was confident that she had enough evidence to make an arrest. She presented her findings to the authorities and waited anxiously for their response.

A few days later, the suspect was taken into custody. Detective Girl was elated but also relieved that the case was finally over. She had poured her heart and soul into it and was happy to see justice served.

As she looked back on the case, she realized how much she had learned and how much she had grown as a detective. She was proud of the work she had done and knew that she had made a difference in the lives of those involved.

Despite the many obstacles and challenges she had faced, Detective Girl had persevered and solved yet another case. She felt confident and ready to take on whatever new challenges lay ahead.

As Detective Girl continued to pursue the potential suspects, she began to face danger and challenges that put her skills and resourcefulness to the test. She received threatening phone calls and was followed by unknown individuals while conducting surveillance. She knew that someone was watching her every move, and it made her anxious.

One day, while staking out a suspect's apartment, Detective Girl saw something she didn't expect. The suspect had a visitor who was carrying a bag that seemed to contain something suspicious. Without hesitation, Detective Girl followed the visitor to a nearby park. She waited until the person was out of sight before she approached the bag.

As she carefully opened it, she realized that it contained several incriminating items related to the case, including documents and photographs. It was a major breakthrough in the case, and it helped Detective Girl get one step closer to cracking it.

However, just as she was about to leave the park, she heard footsteps approaching. She quickly hid behind a tree and saw two men in dark clothing walking towards her. She knew she was in trouble and had to act fast.

With no other options, Detective Girl pulled out her pepper spray and waited for the men to get closer. As they got within range, she sprayed them both, causing them to stumble back in surprise. She took the opportunity to make a run for it, making sure to keep the bag of evidence with her.

Despite the danger she faced, Detective Girl remained determined to crack the case and bring the perpetrators to justice. She knew that the evidence she found was critical, and she needed to act fast to follow up on it before it was too late.

Detective Girl had been pursuing potential suspects for weeks, and she was getting close to cracking the case. However, as she delved deeper into the investigation, she found herself facing more challenges and dangers than ever before.

She had received an anonymous tip that led her to a warehouse on the outskirts of town. It was dark, and the only light came from a few flickering fluorescent bulbs overhead. Detective Girl took a deep breath and cautiously made her way inside, her hand resting on the handle of her pistol.

As she crept through the maze of crates and pallets, she heard footsteps echoing through the warehouse. She froze, pressing herself up against a stack of boxes. Someone was coming.

A figure appeared in the distance, silhouetted against the dim light. Detective Girl squinted, trying to make out their features. As they got closer, she realized it was one of the suspects she had been tracking.

She ducked behind the boxes, trying to stay out of sight. But the suspect had already spotted her. They started running, and Detective Girl took off after them.

She chased the suspect through the maze of crates, dodging obstacles and leaping over piles of debris. Her heart was pounding in her chest, and she could feel her adrenaline surging.

Finally, she caught up to the suspect and tackled them to the ground. They struggled and fought, but Detective Girl was able to subdue them and slap on a pair of handcuffs.

As she led the suspect away, Detective Girl couldn't help but think about how dangerous this case had become. But she knew that she had to keep going, to see it through to the end no matter what the cost.

Detective Girl knew she was close to solving the case, but she also knew that the final stretch would be the most difficult. She had identified the prime suspect, but the evidence was still circumstantial, and she needed more to make an arrest.

She spent hours pouring over every detail of the case, looking for any loose ends that could be tied up. She interviewed witnesses again, reviewed security camera footage, and re-examined physical evidence. She was determined to leave no stone unturned.

But the more she dug, the more she realized that she was up against a dangerous criminal who was willing to do whatever it took to cover their tracks. Detective Girl received anonymous threats and was followed by unknown individuals while working on the case. It was clear that she needed to be more cautious than ever before.

Despite the threats and danger, she continued her investigation, determined to bring the perpetrator to justice. With the help of her colleagues and some innovative techniques, she was able to uncover the crucial piece of evidence that tied the suspect to the crime.

With the case solved, Detective Girl felt a sense of relief, but it was also mixed with a deep sense of sadness for the victims and their families. She knew that the work she did was important, but it was never easy.

As she packed up her things and left the office, she couldn't help but think about the next case she would take on, and the challenges that it would bring. But for now, she allowed herself to savor the moment, knowing that justice had been served.

Detective Girl knew she was getting closer to cracking the case. She had spent countless hours poring over evidence, following up on leads, and chasing down potential suspects. She was determined to bring justice to the victim and their family.

But as she got closer to the truth, the dangers and challenges increased. She received threatening phone calls and suspicious packages at her office. She knew she was getting too close to the culprit, and they were getting desperate to stop her.

Detective Girl knew she had to be careful and use all her skills and resources to solve the case. She called in backup from her fellow detectives and police officers to ensure her safety and to help her gather more evidence.

She worked around the clock, barely sleeping or eating, driven by her passion for justice and her desire to protect others from harm. She felt the weight of the responsibility on her shoulders, knowing that the victim and their family were counting on her to bring the perpetrator to justice.

As she worked, she reflected on the lessons she had learned from previous cases, reminding herself to stay focused and objective, to trust her instincts, and to never give up. She knew that this case would be one of the toughest she had ever faced, but she was determined to see it through to the end.

SOLVING THE CASE

With her skills and determination, Detective Girl was finally able to crack the case. She had followed up on every lead and pursued every potential suspect until she had enough evidence to bring the culprit to justice.
It was a long and difficult journey, but she had finally done it. She felt a sense of satisfaction and relief as she handed over

the evidence to the authorities, knowing that justice would be served.

The culprit was arrested and taken into custody, and the community was grateful to Detective Girl for solving the case. She had once again proven herself to be an invaluable member of the community, and her dedication to her work had not gone unnoticed.

As she reflected on the case, Detective Girl felt a sense of pride and accomplishment. She had used all her skills and resources to solve the mystery and bring the culprit to justice. It was a reminder of why she had become a detective in the first place, and why she loved her job.

But even as she celebrated her victory, Detective Girl knew that there would be more cases to come. She would always be on the lookout for new mysteries to solve, and she was ready to take on whatever challenges lay ahead. For Detective Girl, there was no greater thrill than the pursuit of justice.

As Detective Girl brought the culprit to justice, she couldn't help but feel a sense of satisfaction. Another mystery had been solved, and justice had been served. She handed over the culprit to the authorities, and they were taken away in handcuffs.

The case was finally closed, and Detective Girl could breathe a sigh of relief. She had worked hard to solve the case, and she felt proud of what she had accomplished.

But as she walked away from the police station, Detective Girl couldn't shake the feeling that something was off. She felt a sense of emptiness that she couldn't quite explain.

As she pondered her feelings, Detective Girl realized that she was beginning to feel burnt out. She had been working non-stop on the case for weeks, and it had taken a toll on her emotionally and physically.

She knew that she needed to take some time to recharge, so she decided to take a break from work for a while. She spent time with her family and friends, and she enjoyed the simple pleasures of life.

After a few weeks, Detective Girl felt rejuvenated and ready to take on new challenges. She returned to work with a renewed sense of purpose and a fresh perspective.

The community was grateful for her service, and they honored her for her hard work and dedication to keeping them safe. Detective Girl felt proud of her accomplishments and grateful for the support of her community.

As she looked back on the cases she had solved, Detective Girl realized that each one had taught her valuable lessons. She had grown as a detective and as a person, and she knew that she was ready for whatever challenges lay ahead.

After successfully solving the case, Detective Girl felt a sense of relief mixed with accomplishment. She knew that justice had been served and that she had made a difference in the lives of those affected by the crime.

As she sat in her office, surrounded by the evidence and notes from the case, Detective Girl began to reflect on the lessons she had learned. She realized that each case was unique and required a different approach. She learned that the key to solving a case was not just about following the evidence, but also about understanding the motives and intentions of those involved.

She also recognized that the emotional toll of working on such cases was not something to be ignored. She knew that it was important to take time to process the trauma and grief that often came with these situations.

But most of all, Detective Girl was grateful for the opportunity to make a positive impact in her community. She knew that her work as a detective had helped to bring peace to those affected by crime and that her efforts had made her city a safer place to live.

As she sat there, lost in thought, Detective Girl was interrupted by a knock on her door. It was her captain, there to congratulate her on another successful case. He praised her for her hard work, dedication, and bravery.

The captain then presented Detective Girl with a medal of honor, recognizing her service to the community. Detective Girl felt proud and honored, but she knew that it was not just about the recognition. She was motivated by a deep desire to make a difference and help those in need.

As she looked at the medal, Detective Girl knew that there were more cases to solve and more challenges to overcome. She was ready to face whatever came her way, armed with the skills, experience, and determination to make a difference.

As Detective Girl reflects on the case, she realizes the emotional toll it has taken on her. She remembers the sleepless nights, the constant worry, and the stress that came with trying to solve the case.

However, despite the difficulties, she takes pride in the fact that she was able to bring justice to those who had been wronged. She thinks about the impact she's made in the community and how her work has helped bring peace to those who have suffered.

She also thinks about the lessons she's learned throughout her work as a detective. She knows now the importance of patience, perseverance, and attention to detail. She realizes that sometimes, it's not just about solving the case but also about helping those who have been affected by it.

As she takes a deep breath and looks back at her accomplishments, she feels a sense of fulfillment knowing that she is making a difference in the world.

Detective Girl leaned back in her chair, feeling a sense of satisfaction and accomplishment. She had solved the case, and the culprit was now behind bars. The relief of bringing justice to the victim's family and putting the perpetrator away was overwhelming.

She couldn't help but reflect on the journey she had gone through to get to this point. The long hours spent piecing together the evidence, the challenges faced along the way, and the moments of doubt when she wasn't sure if she would be able to solve the case. But now, all that was behind her, and she had succeeded.

As she looked around her office, she realized that this was exactly where she was meant to be. Her passion for helping people and bringing justice to those who deserved it had driven her to become a detective, and it was moments like these that made it all worthwhile.

She knew that there would always be more cases, more challenges to face, and more obstacles to overcome. But she was ready for whatever came her way. Detective Girl was a force to be reckoned with, and she had proven that she was more than capable of handling anything that came her way.

As she left her office and walked out into the city, she felt a sense of pride in the work she had accomplished. She knew that her efforts had made a difference, and that was all that mattered. The world was a better place because of her work, and that thought alone filled her with a sense of satisfaction and pride.

As Detective Girl looks back on the case, she feels a sense of satisfaction and accomplishment. She knows that her hard work and determination paid off, and that justice has been served. She thinks about the victim and their family, and how her actions have helped bring them closure and peace of mind.

But Detective Girl also realizes that her work is never done. There will always be more cases to solve, more mysteries to unravel, and more people in need of her help. She feels a sense of responsibility to continue using her skills and resources to make a difference in her community.

As she reflects on the lessons she's learned, Detective Girl realizes the importance of perseverance, critical thinking, and empathy. She understands that every case is different, and that there is no one-size-fits-all approach to solving crimes.

She also knows that it's important to maintain a sense of compassion and understanding, even in the face of the most heinous crimes.

Despite the emotional toll that her work can take, Detective Girl is grateful for the opportunity to make a positive impact in the world. She knows that her work is important, and that she has the skills and determination to make a real difference. As she looks ahead to the future, she feels a sense of excitement and anticipation for the challenges and opportunities that lie ahead.

MOVING FORWARD

Detective Girl sat at her desk, deep in thought. She had just solved another case, bringing justice to those who had been wronged. It was moments like this that made her job worthwhile.

As she reflected on her career, she thought back to all the cases she had solved. Each one was unique and presented its own set of challenges. Some cases were straightforward, while others required her to dig deeper and use all of her skills and resources.

She thought about the time she had to chase down a group of bank robbers who had been terrorizing the city. She remembered the adrenaline pumping through her veins as she pursued them through the busy streets, eventually cornering them and bringing them to justice.

Then there was the case of the missing child, where she had to use her wits and resourcefulness to track down the kidnapper and rescue the child. That case had taken an emotional toll on her, but she had persevered, knowing that the safety of the child was at stake.

As she continued to reflect, Detective Girl realized that she had grown as a person and as a detective through each case. She had learned to think outside the box, to use her instincts and intuition, and to never give up, even when the odds were against her.

She also thought about the people she had helped along the way. The victims of crimes who had finally received justice, the families who had been reunited, and the community as a whole who felt safer knowing that she was on the case.

Despite the challenges and dangers she faced on a daily basis, Detective Girl knew that she had found her calling. She loved the rush of solving a case, the satisfaction of bringing closure to those affected by crime, and the sense of pride she felt in making a difference in the world.

With a smile on her face, she knew that she was ready for whatever challenges lay ahead. She would continue to serve and protect her community, using all of her skills and resources to bring justice to those who deserved it.

As Detective Girl reflects on the cases she's solved and the challenges she's faced, she realizes that being a detective is not just a job, it's a way of life. She has learned so much from each case, and it has made her a better person.

One of the most important things she has learned is to never give up, even when things seem impossible. She has faced challenges that seemed insurmountable, but she never let them defeat her. Instead, she faced them head-on and found a way to overcome them.

Another thing she has learned is the value of teamwork. She used to think that she could do everything on her own, but she soon realized that she couldn't solve a case without the help of others. Whether it was her colleagues in the police department or the community members who provided tips and information, she needed their support to succeed.

Detective Girl also learned the importance of staying calm and focused in high-pressure situations. She has had to deal with dangerous criminals, distraught families, and fast-moving investigations, but she has learned to stay level-headed and make rational decisions, even in the most stressful of circumstances.

Finally, Detective Girl has learned to appreciate the impact that her work has on the community. She has seen firsthand how her actions can change lives and bring justice to those who have been wronged. It is a responsibility that she takes seriously and is proud to uphold.

As she reflects on these lessons, Detective Girl realizes that being a detective is not just about solving cases; it's about making a difference in people's lives. She feels a sense of fulfillment and purpose in her work and knows that she is making a positive impact on the world.

After reflecting on her past cases and the challenges she's faced, Detective Girl realized that she had accomplished so much but still had so much to learn. She was determined to continue her education and training so that she could become an even better detective.

She began to research courses and programs that would help her advance her skills and knowledge. She reached out to mentors and colleagues for advice and guidance. Detective Girl knew that she needed to stay up-to-date with the latest techniques and technologies in order to stay ahead of the game.

As she set her sights on new goals for her career, Detective Girl also wanted to make sure she was taking care of herself. She knew that the job could be emotionally taxing, and that she needed to find ways to stay balanced and healthy. She began to prioritize self-care practices like exercise, meditation, and spending time with loved ones.

With her renewed sense of purpose and dedication, Detective Girl was ready to take on whatever challenges lay ahead. She felt grateful for the opportunity to make a difference in people's lives, and she was excited to continue her work as a detective.

on her past cases and the impact she has made, Detective Girl begins to set new goals for herself and her career. She feels a renewed sense of purpose and motivation to continue her work in solving crimes and helping the community.

She decides to expand her knowledge and skills by enrolling in advanced training courses and workshops to improve her investigative techniques and stay up-to-date with the latest advancements in technology and forensics.

In addition to professional development, Detective Girl also wants to focus on personal growth. She realizes the importance of taking care of her mental and physical health to maintain a balance in her life. She starts to prioritize self-care practices such as meditation, exercise, and spending quality time with loved ones.

Furthermore, she wants to give back to her community by volunteering her time and skills to help those in need. She researches local organizations and nonprofits that align with her values and goals and begins to look for ways to get involved.

As she sets new goals for herself, Detective Girl also reflects on the impact she wants to make in the world. She wants to inspire others to pursue their passions and make a difference in their own way. She starts to share her experiences and insights through speaking engagements and mentorship programs, hoping to empower the next generation of crime solvers.

With her new goals and aspirations, Detective Girl is excited for the future and all the possibilities that lie ahead. She knows that there will be challenges and setbacks along the way, but she is confident that with hard work and dedication, she can make a positive impact and continue to serve her community with passion and purpose.

As Detective Girl reflects on her career and the cases she's solved, she realizes that there is so much more she wants to accomplish. She's proud of the work she's done so far, but she knows there are still many challenges and obstacles ahead.

With a renewed sense of purpose, she sets new goals for herself and her career. She wants to continue to serve her community and make a difference in people's lives. She wants to become an even better detective and develop new skills that will help her solve even more complex cases.

As she looks to the future with hope and determination, she knows that there will be setbacks and failures along the way. But she also knows that with hard work and perseverance, she can overcome any challenge and achieve her goals.

She's grateful for the support of her colleagues, friends, and family, who have been there for her throughout her career. And she knows that she wouldn't be where she is today without their help and encouragement.

With a sense of excitement and anticipation, Detective Girl prepares to embark on the next chapter of her career. She knows that there will be ups and downs, but she's ready to face whatever comes her way with courage and determination.

Detective Girl sat at her desk, looking out the window as she contemplated her next move. She had come a long way since her first case, and now she was a respected member of the department, known for her sharp intuition and tenacity.

As she reflected on the past cases she had solved and the challenges she had faced, she felt a sense of pride in herself. She had overcome many obstacles and had worked tirelessly to bring justice to those who had been wronged.

But she knew that her work was far from over. There were still many cases to be solved, and many people who needed her help. She thought about the goals she had set for herself, and the steps she needed to take to achieve them. She knew that it wouldn't be easy, but she was determined to do whatever it took to succeed.

As she looked to the future, she felt a sense of hope. She knew that there would be more challenges ahead, but she was ready to face them head-on. She knew that with hard work and determination, she could make a real difference in the world.

With a deep breath, Detective Girl stood up from her desk and made her way out of the office. She was ready to take on whatever came her way, and she knew that she had the skills and the determination to succeed. As she walked out into the bright sunshine, she felt a sense of purpose and a renewed sense of passion for her work. She was ready to make a difference, one case at a time.

CONCLUSION

As the book comes to a close, the reader is left with a sense of awe and inspiration at Detective Girl's journey. She has faced numerous challenges, both professionally and personally, but has come out stronger and more determined than ever before.

Reflecting on her journey, Detective Girl acknowledges that solving cases is not just about intelligence or skill, but about having empathy and compassion for the victims and their families. She also realizes the importance of having a strong support system, both at work and in her personal life, to help her through the tough times.

Despite the many obstacles she's faced, Detective Girl remains hopeful and determined, looking towards the future with optimism and a sense of purpose. She sets new goals for herself and her career, determined to continue making a difference in the lives of those she serves.

As the final pages turn, the reader is left with a sense of admiration for Detective Girl and the many others like her, who work tirelessly to make the world a better and safer place. The journey may be difficult, but as Detective Girl has shown, it is also incredibly rewarding.

The book concludes with a final reflection on Detective Girl's journey. As she looks back on her career, she feels a deep sense of pride for the work she has done and the people she has helped. She knows that being a detective is not an easy job, but it is one that brings great rewards.

Throughout her journey, Detective Girl has faced many challenges and obstacles. She has had to navigate complex cases, work with difficult people, and confront her own fears and limitations. But through it all, she has remained focused and determined, always striving to do her best and make a positive impact.

As she looks to the future, Detective Girl knows that there will be more challenges ahead. She knows that the work of a detective is never done, and that there will always be cases that need to be solved and people that need her help. But she is ready for whatever comes her way, knowing that she has the skills, the experience, and the determination to face whatever challenges lie ahead.

The book ends with a message of hope and inspiration for all those who aspire to be detectives, or who are simply looking to make a positive impact in their communities. Detective Girl's journey is a testament to the power of hard work, perseverance, and a deep sense of purpose. It is a reminder that no matter how difficult the road may be, there is always a way forward, and always a way to make a difference.

As the final chapter draws to a close, the reader is left with a feeling of satisfaction and closure. The journey of Detective Girl, her struggles, her triumphs, and her growth throughout the cases have been fully explored. The story has shown the importance of perseverance, hard work, and the ability to overcome obstacles, no matter how daunting they may seem.

The reader has watched Detective Girl tackle challenging cases, face danger and obstacles, and emerge victorious through her unwavering determination and skill. They have seen her solve seemingly impossible cases and bring justice to victims and their families.

As the book concludes, the reader is left with a sense of admiration for Detective Girl and her work. They have witnessed the impact she has made on the community and the difference she has made in the lives of those around her.

The book leaves the reader with a sense of hope and inspiration, knowing that there are people like Detective Girl in the world who are committed to making a difference and upholding justice. It is a fitting conclusion to an inspiring story, and the reader is sure to close the book with a newfound appreciation for the work of detectives and law enforcement professionals.

As the final chapter comes to a close, the reader is left with a sense of closure and satisfaction. Detective Girl has solved numerous cases and overcome a variety of challenges and obstacles. The reader has followed her journey through the ups and downs, the successes and failures, and watched as she has grown and developed as a detective.

Throughout the book, the reader has seen Detective Girl tackle cases with determination, using her intelligence and resourcefulness to solve even the most difficult of cases. She has faced danger and challenges head-on, always determined to bring justice to those who need it.

As the final chapter concludes, the reader can't help but feel a sense of admiration for Detective Girl's dedication and bravery. They have seen her evolve as a detective and as a person, overcoming personal struggles and pushing herself to new heights.

The book leaves the reader with a sense of hope and inspiration, encouraging them to face their own challenges with the same determination and resolve as Detective Girl. It is a story of perseverance, resilience, and the power of the human spirit, leaving the reader with a renewed sense of optimism for the future.

As the book comes to a close, Detective Girl's story is not over. While she has solved the cases that were presented in this book, there is still much to be explored in her world of crime-solving and investigation.

The final pages of the book hint at new mysteries and challenges that await Detective Girl in the future

Printed in France by Amazon
Brétigny-sur-Orge, FR